# THE MIRROR

## TATE ADAMS

*AuthorHouse*™
*1663 Liberty Drive*
*Bloomington, IN 47403*
*www.authorhouse.com*
*Phone: 1-800-839-8640*

*© 2010 Tate Adams. All rights reserved.*

*No part of this book may be reproduced, stored in a retrieval system, or transmitted by any means without the written permission of the author.*

*First published by AuthorHouse 7/22/2010*

*ISBN: 978-1-4520-5258-8 (sc)*
*ISBN: 978-1-4520-6280-8(e)*

*Printed in the United States of America*

*This book is printed on acid-free paper.*

*Because of the dynamic nature of the Internet, any Web addresses or links contained in this book may have changed since publication and may no longer be valid. The views expressed in this work are solely those of the author and do not necessarily reflect the views of the publisher, and the publisher hereby disclaims any responsibility for them.*

# CONTENTS

The Mirror ................................................................... 1
My Birthday ................................................................ 14
The Evening Out ......................................................... 27
The incarnation .......................................................... 32
The wooden box ........................................................ 35
Stephan ..................................................................... 41
The other room ......................................................... 44
The Diary ................................................................... 47
The Coffee Shop ........................................................ 53
The hospital ............................................................... 58
The library ................................................................. 66
The Card Game .......................................................... 77
His other room .......................................................... 82
Charles at the coffee shop ......................................... 90
The Séance ................................................................ 98
The Raid .................................................................. 105
The stairwell ............................................................ 128
The Medium ............................................................ 139
The Hospital ............................................................ 143
The house on the common ..................................... 171
The brewery ............................................................ 188
The big band ........................................................... 195
The common ........................................................... 204
The Zoo ................................................................... 208
Churchill .................................................................. 219
The Bag ................................................................... 229
The Snow ................................................................ 233

# THE MIRROR

I bought it from a flea market sale along the South Bank, under the shadow of the National Theatre. The lady I purchased it from was a little unusually spooky, not the mad hippy type you usually saw haunting around there. Her attire was the remnants of some ancient hippy mixed with gypsy frozen in time. She had thanked me for purchasing the mirror and whispered something about superstitions. When I handed her the cash, she remarked, "Do you wonder how many tales it could tell if it could speak?" She smiled creepily as she greedily snatched the money from my hand. "How many faces have looked into that mirror? How many years has it reflected back, not questioning the viewer, asking nothing but to be kept clean?" A wry smile and quirky laugh echoed under the pass way.

It was ugly. It was bulbous, unloved, and probably had been hanging in some greasy old pub toilet for decades. The thought of it viewing the many rituals of men playing fireman with their swinging appendages sent a shudder down my spine. The scene had to be blocked from my mind, and I laughed aloud with the old kook. I trudged it home, stopping on occasion to ease the weight of it, wondering whether my Wonder Woman superhuman strength that I initially had on first lifting it would endure the journey.

It was, I recall, an art nouveau or deco style with a carved arched wooden frame embracing the glass. It appeared to have had some paint work on the carvings, but it was blistered away. There were only faint speckles of paint that probably had splashed onto the wood whilst it was hung as the wall was painted. Some of the mirror's silver backing had lifted, and the glass was chipped in small areas around the periphery.

But I loved it for its chunky maleness; I could smell the waft of Old Spice and Samson tobacco, but nothing of the gent's public-house loo. It was perfect for my apartment, which happened to be art deco, a real old 1920s Charleston, revisited and renovated.

There was only place for me to hang it, on the opposite wall to the fireplace the pride of place, of course. A centre piece for idle chit-chat and to reflect the shimmering, dirty Thames back through my balcony window

I won the flat through some damned competition at the airport while going to Barcelona for a mad girls' weekend. It was a fluke, you'd say. There would be no other way I could have afforded such a luxurious location. I was told to make a rich buck by selling the place or letting it, but I fell in love with the location and the amazing décor: the windows with their colourful motifs and immaculate iron castings; the main entrance with its heavy walnut double doors, marble floors, and cast-iron cats as guardians to the building; its grand, open staircase with a swirl of colourful chandeliers ,a scene from many early black-and-white flicks;

the supporting pillars with carved-stone creeping leafs, splashed with an array of blues and greens, a wonderment of the precise passion of the stone mansion. Not many neighbours, however secretive, polite, quiet, and demur. Many of the apartments had been knocked through in the '60s to make them huge penthouse suites – exclusive, elitist, upper-crust, perhaps. I know that one such neighbour was a Member of Parliament; another was a wealthy club owner. But they kept themselves to themselves. The concierge was always polite, always informal, but I always managed a smile and a chit-chat about them as a person rather than a subservient machine to be barked at. The janitor lived in a small apartment, purposely built in the basement. He was in high demand by the wealthier established residents. As I understood it, the competition for my flat was not a welcome prize, but it had been done to raise funds to keep up the perfect maintenance of this listed building in such times of financial recession. It was a relief to some residents to have a nurse on the presence, but others pooh-poohed the idea of a single, working-class female in such a grand location. My main discrimination came from the ladies that were associated with the wealthier gents. Perhaps they saw me as competition, bimbo-like. But they were just self centred heartless snobs who never had to lift a plate from a table, let alone clean up the rear end of a dying patient.

I resolved some of that chilling embrace by riding in on my white charger and saving the MP's fingers from the jaws of his meat shredder. His lady-friend had come banging hard on my door one late night near last Christmas in a fit of panic. His apartment was on the opposite side of the hallway.

The hallway had sparkling lighting, art-deco chandeliers, brightly coloured muse murals, and flamboyant pillars of greens, blues, and gold's. The floor was chequered in motif tiles and had neatly tucked-in soft-coloured carpet running through the middle. It was truly a marvel and the only other place I had seen so gladly decorated was the National Gallery on Trafalgar Square.

I was tucking into my second glass of Lindeman's chardonnay still in full uniform from a strenuous shift at the A&E. A young boy had been gang-stabbed—that was a bloody sight, we almost lost the poor lad. The gang had burst into the unit seeking to finish him off, but the police and security had been involved. It almost turned to a war zone. Thankfully our crisis training was seriously tested, and we passed apparently with a green light.

The MP did lose the tips on two of his digits. But Uncle gave him the best service at the A&E department, paging in Dr Omar, the specialist reconstructive surgeon. Dr Omar did a real fine job on repairing what was left of the digits. He suggested artificial extensions if the cosmetic end-result was too unsightly. The MP declined, and red-faced now, he has a pro cook in-house to sort out his dining needs. He did request my discreetness in the matter. And, of course, I obliged gracefully. I did enquire why he had not used the guard on the shredder, and you can all but imagine the retorting remark!. I guess some folks are best left to being creative with words and heated discussions rather than dabbling in to the fine arts of culinary delights and cookery gadgets.

## THE MIRROR

It was a once-in-a-lifetime chance of living somewhere so grand.

The view spanned from upriver to downriver. You can see past Tower Bridge, right along Battersea power station, the Gherkin, St Paul's, the Eye, down to Parliament, and beyond. It was spectacular and amazing to watch the river rise and fall on its own, a beastly sleeping dragon. It was so tranquil at times, and yet venomous at others, taking unsuspected travellers or workers as sea nymphs snatching their prey. If you fall in, there are good chances they will find you up by the Dartford Crossing days later. It demanded respect at the utmost, with the swirl of changing currents and busy river traffic. However, there was something so beautiful about the water and its once clear, clean, life-giving source and its amazing route to and from the sea to maintain trade and nourishment of the local settlers.

I had slowly redecorated the flat over the past eighteen months to give it a real comfy Charleston feel of my own. It was a long slog, in between shift work and permission granting the alterations of this listed building. It was all worth the effort. Some of my handiwork was less desirable, but it satisfied the local authorities. Of course, professionals would be hired for some points, for example unblocking and restoring the bricked-up fireplace to its near-as-possible original condition, with its immense, foreboding stone features and stacked hearth. Uncle had helped finance the restoration as an investment, and of course to use the flat for entertaining, to impress new investors or high society clientele. I didn't mind; it was always well–cleaned and my fridge and wine cellar well-stocked afterwards as a thank you. The first smoky pine logs crackling away on that hearth were a joy, cheering the chilly, grey, damp London winter night.

I get many visitors and never have a problem getting a house sitter when I go on vacation. Rules are set, and I inform the janitor and concierge. I am very independent and know exactly if someone is on the chat up for the wrong reasons. It has happened. I don't have money, but I guess I have luck.

I hung the mirror on the Thursday evening two days prior to my birthday. I had extensively cleaned, polished, and made it sparkle with all the love I could pour onto it. It was a magnificent art piece. It was so immense and foreboding it was obvious that was the only place to hang it.

I sat outside on my balcony observing the slush of the spring rain bounce around on the pavement and swirl the river waters. Of course, like every decent human being that works hard all day with the public, I required a large glass of Lindeman's chardonnay. The breeze gusted, twirling, and playing with my hair until I resembled an ancient banshee.

I drained my glass and proceeded to refill it. The bottle empty, I entered back into the flat and across the living room toward the wine-chill cabinet by the dining table. I was part way across the living room when the reflection in the mirror drew my attention. I shrugged my shoulders, raised my glass to it, and bellowed, "Cheers. Drinks on me. Happy birthday!"

That was my first encounter with the mirror. While imagining living as a spinster in an old building with an old mirror and being partly intoxicated, I swear I saw a face, not mine, but a face in the mirror. The thing is, it didn't creep me out. I liked the face; it seemed gentle, perhaps sad around the eyes, hard-worked, masculine, lost. I liked it, so sad for me to say I have a phantom that I could talk to – a ghost in the glass.

It was Friday night that Johnnie rang me, to inform me that he couldn't make my birthday. He said it was because he had to go to Germany on business, that an important deal was going down and he couldn't possibly miss such a fantastic offer due to the current financial crisis. Yes, I thought, something always comes up. It was my suspicion that he was messing around with my old flatmate, Carolina, the tart, always clambering over other girls' guys. My guess was that he got cheap tickets from Ryan air, where the old tart worked, and was off to the beer festival over in Deutschland, the city of Berlin with the tart or his sleazy buddies. Anyhow, that was the end of our relationship, the straw that broke the camel's back. Fantastic, a very happy birthday! I threw down my mobile in disgust and burst into tears, feeling like a fool for having been part of this man's attempt to get his foot in the door of my investment, and yet he still has no respect for any female. Johnnie is a heartless prick. I played the fool to his charms and outlandish swooning. I was a fool an idiot, to believe he would be loyal, even when Tart Air was wandering her eyes over him, using the huge firepower of her double-d bra cup size that no man could resist a peak at. He would be at the flat before me, sipping cups of coffee and dunking biscuits rather erotically with Tart Air. He soon started paying attention to me again when I moved into King George House alone. But my instincts were to cool it as much as possible, but I couldn't let go because of my own damned insecurities, my fear of being lonely and the old time bomb inside me saying, "You're not getting any younger, Samantha."

So what does any recently dumped girl do on the night before her birthday? Ring up an old, reliable friend, get some sad movie out, and make it an excuse to bawl your eyes out. Well, that is exactly what I did.

Simon came round with two bottles of Lindeman's chardonnay, a bottle of fizz (good Spanish cava), and the movie *Big Fish*. He hugged me so tight when he burst through my front door carrying an armful of flowers tangled up with carrier bags of plonk, Haagen-Dazs ice cream, and a box of tissues. Simon, I have to say, is as camp as Butlins and is a fab gay friend.

We slagged off Johnnie, and Simon kept ranting on about how he was going to scratch out Johnnie's eyes the next time he meets him. We sat comforting each other; we wept at the movie, stuffing our faces with ice cream until our bellies were so full we were almost sick. We lit the smoky pine-scented hearth and let the night crackle away our worries.

Simon paused the movie to use the bathroom. He is a very particular well-presented guy — smart, articulate, and damn gorgeous. He loves films, books, and most of the population. He does have issues with scruffy, baggy-bummed jeans wearers and gang attitudes. He thinks that there is always another way to resolve issues and violence is not an option. However, he did step in that night at A&E when the gang crashed through the unit. His tall, muscular, fit frame ran down one member with a hardened rugby tackle. He did it with such ease, but afterwards shrugged off the ease of it. I recall he said something along the lines of, "Well, when you go to an all-boys private school and some fellow keeps pushing you about 'cause you're a sissy, you join the rugby team, learn to defend yourself, and pack a real hard punch in the visage of your bully. Mmm, breaking his nose, making him even uglier, while I keep my good looks. And it's all legal on the rugby field. As long as the ref doesn't see," he would laugh.

Simon stood up from the sofa and stumbled onto wobbly legs and a frozen gluteus. He wobbled over to pause at the mirror, remarking at its imposing visage but chic oddity. He stroked his fingers lightly across the top arch, caressing the wood grain, testing for dust, probably, knowing Simon. He gazed into the glass, gently stroking his fingers through his well-groomed hair. Then his body tightened at his gaze; he stood frozen, staring into his reflection. Holding his breath, he pushed his face closer to the mirror. His eyes widened with amazement. I watched him carefully touch the mirror's glass. He gave a nervous laugh. "Who's the tasty guy in the mirror? Very clever imaging. Where did you get it?" He didn't take his eyes off the image.

I stood up and almost toppled over. I squinted my eyes across the room to try to view the image. Simon didn't move his glare. Without warning, Simon began flapping his arms. "He's moving! Where's he going? Where's hunkster going? Quick, come see." He beckoned urgently..

I raced across the room, crashing over the empty bottles and cartons, but the face was gone.

Simon pressed his nose up against the glass again. "I swear, I swear I saw a man, a real gorge. I did! I did!" At that point, I thought Simon was going to implode, with his hands flapping and his head twitching from one side to the other.

He had, of course, completely forgotten about his bladder's needs, which worried me with all the excitement erupting from every ounce of his body.

"Yes," I paused slyly, "I know. I think we met the other night." I admitted. Simon flicked his head around at me and put his hands on his hips in disdain.

"What!" he couldn't sound angry or scary if he tried really hard.

"Last night, actually. Didn't get a real good look. Just a glimpse." I shrugged.

"You've got a man in your mirror, and you didn't tell me? Wow, how exciting. Have you given him a name?" his reactions were mixed.

I shrugged my shoulders. "I haven't got a good look at the ghost. What did he look like?"

"Clark Kent in a porn movie! God, horny!"

"Simon, please..."

He was getting overenthusiastic. He viewed the mirror again with some intensity and lifted it away from the wall to see if there was anything hidden behind it. Just my bad decorating. Simon then reacted in a way unfamiliar to me: he almost dropped the mirror in frustration. In quick reprimand, he accused me of winding him up. He asked me in his best Gestapo impression, "So girlfriend... where did you buy it? Hmm? What cunning little venture? Hmmm? Been up the King's Road, have we? Hmm?" His hands were now back on his hips. He sauntered from one foot to the other, glaring at me. "I come around here... and you wind me up with some...." he then slavered, "some hunkster in the looking glass? One of those moving images that can be projected, hmmm? Very funny, girlfriend!"

I think too much alcohol and the emotional turmoil of Johnnie and the ghost in the mirror were becoming all a little too much for sensitive Simon. I offered a coffee to chill him out. He felt too emotionally unstable and left after doing his ablutions His arms were still flapping about, and he was going from laughter to tears all in one movement.

When he left, I returned to the mirror and was shocked with what I saw. I viewed my own reflection, but the backdrop was not the same décor as my flat. My eyes were smudgy from weeping at the film and a little red from the wine. The TV and cosy sofa were missing. A chesterfield two-seater was plonked in front of the iron fireplace, and a scooped walnut sideboard was wedged between the chimney breast and balcony window. On top of it was a large old-fashioned wireless radio. Yes, a wireless. It was so bulky it would probably take two of me to lift. It had a large clock face backlit with a huge dial. There was a rotating pointing needle to display the stations. Between the lit iron fireplace and the chesterfield was a small table with swirling tobacco smoke, which come from roll-ups. The room was dimly lit from wall sconces and a rather tall cast-iron lamp, which was behind the chesterfield. There appeared to have a sort of drink cabinet placed in front of the mirror, which I could see by looking directly down into the glass. As I peered across the room, I could work out the back of the ghost's head. His hair was dark, neatly parted, waxed, and combed to one side. Squinting my eyes up, I saw that his hair was slightly wavy by the way it kinked down into his nape. The strong aroma of Old Spice, Samson tobacco came through again. I breathed in a sharp breath at the scene.

"Jesus, I am losing the plot, broke up with a sleazeball, and now I'm imagining ghosts in my mirror."

Just as my thought was provoked, the head on the sofa turned and looked straight at me, smiled, gave a wink, blew me a kiss, and raised his large brandy glass to me. I froze, squinting at the face. Dapper is a word I'd say to describe him, not quite Clark Kent in porn. I responded oddly again, catching the gesture of the blown kiss. My feet were cemented to the carpet. I tried desperately to wiggle my toes. I was terrified, yet thrilled to be experiencing this, and I swore never to eat so much Häagen Dazs ever again.

He turned back to gaze into the fireplace. He was writing something in a leather-bound book. He was also tapping the table to a rhythm or beat I assumed was emitting from the radio. I felt uncomfortable to spy any further and finally found release for my feet. When I turned into my room, an eerie sensation crept over me. A realisation of how old the building was, it's past, it's grandness, its relentless history, amazed me. I smiled deep within my soul to be a part of this building and its development and its history. My room was how it should be, with the spillage of empty cartons, bottles, and a frozen HD screen with Ewan McGregor's face frozen on it.

Deciding that the evening had gone well and that my head was too tired and spinny to care about tidying the mess we had made, I turned off Ewan McGregor and called it a night.

I washed my face with cold water in the bathroom, the aromatic mixture of tobacco and Old Spice wafted everywhere. It was almost rancid, choking me. I gave Simon a quick call to see if he was okay. He said he had a headache and we would chat tomorrow, reassuring me that we would be coming out to the Chinese in Soho as promised ,because that sleazeball who he'd liked to scratch the eyes out of had been such a bastard to me on my birthday.

I didn't sleep much. The waft of the tobacco was overwhelming.

# MY BIRTHDAY

I awoke early, and it being my birthday, I was allowed to be off duty. The staff nurse had arranged me to have some me-time and told me to chill out for a few days. My hangover had not quite kicked in, so I downed a few ibuprofen, chucked on my trainers, scraped back my hair into a straggled ponytail, wired up to my iPod, and went for a run. I know that Simon was tinkering around with my iPod last week. I let him reload the music because I am pretty impatient and, to be honest, was never really quite sure where to download the music to get the best sound or best price. I was in for a surprise. He said that my taste in music needed expanding and that I shouldn't just listen to Oasis or Coldplay all the time.

I took the stairs down for quick warm-up. No problem, I was getting quite quick, leaping a few steps at a time. The concierge is used to my bedraggled, mad running attire and me prancing through the foyer, smiling that knowing smile that in a few hours time I will be red-faced, sweaty, and clutching some form of beverage and a roll.

The usual route I took was across London Bridge, with the

famous HMS *Belfast* to the right of it, still sturdy, a reminder of the British valiantly sinking the German *Scharnhorst* in December 1943 during World War II. It was now a military floating museum for enthusiasts.

I ran up towards the monument, but took the steps down onto the bank of the Thames, past the Institute of Engineering and Technology and its Victorian building. The first stone was laid by Queen Victoria on 24th March 1886. It was originally then a hospital of the Royal Colleges of Physicians. It was a magnificent building and still had the original marble flooring in the main foyer entrance.

Down along the Thames walk path, amongst other mad runners, some with their wired heart monitors, others running in packs, most all tuned up with their headphones, my iPod album changed to U2 *How to Dismantle an Atomic Bomb*

I trudged up towards Parliament and the embankment, passing Queenhithe dock. The dock dates back as far as AD 886 when the former roman city was recaptured by King Alfred the Great. It stopped being used as a dock for selling grain and foodstuffs in the fifteenth century because it couldn't cope with the amount of trade. So trading started down at Billingsgate.

The tide is in, so no one is mud- larking down on the beach. I don't know why they do that anyway, I only saw plastic bottles and beer cans washed up when the tide goes out! My body starts to slow, not willing to go further, knowing that it would be some time before it would stop. I grit my stubborn mind and pushed through the pain barrier.

The tracks are surprisingly good. Simon did a grand job. Some real old stuff from British '80s and some from the '70s.

I missed out on some of the '90s stuff, being out in South Africa. "Pig Bag" started playing, giving a better rhythm to my stride.

I duck down under the Queen's House and out in front of the Globe View apartments. Some of the modern buildings that were being constructed were pretty bizarre, all shiny glass fronts, solid concrete walls, space-age stuff. However, some constructions were done really neatly, as if they had been there for two centuries or more. Very clever. It was pretty difficult to see what is new. I turned into Broken Wharf and some mad track came on, I think Simon called it "Procal Harum A whiter shade of pale". I went up onto Paul's Walk and then it changed to "Don't Stop Me Now" By Queen.

I waved my hands towards St Paul's, giving it a cheer for surviving most of the twentieth and so far twenty-first century. I gained a few quirky glances from passers-by, but, hey, I wasn't a stiff-upper-lipped Brit!

I went under the Millennium Bridge and past the famous Millennium Sundial.

My eyes spot HMS *President (1918)* along the embankment, and the music shifted to Frank Sinatra.

I went past Kings Reach and HQS *Wellington*. Wow, fancy having an old steamboat for your headquarters like the Honourable Company of Master Mariners.

Temple Pier was next, and the tourist buses were rumbling past, some left-hand drive, German or Spanish – wow, to come all the way from Spain on a coach. How tedious that would be. Mind you, I have had friends go to the Costa Brava, by means of coach. A three-day hike through the French auto route, but the bus had its restrictor set at sixty mph, how boring. Then a windy tent to rest your bones in and cold showers only. Brr, not for me. I like my hot, steamy baths, not being stuck on a bus for three days with a bunch of strangers. I go away to get away from people. I want a pool, a bar, a hot bath, clean, crisp sheets, and the freedom to come and go. The aviation industry was a revolution of society. It's convenient and now cheaper than ever, except for the taxes they all bung on top now.

I passed the *Queen Mary* floating restaurant. I had great fun and memories of the World Cup in there with a bunch of mad Italian tourists. That was a funny evening. The thing is, it has its own history like so many things in London. It was an original steam ship on the Clyde, ferrying passengers and mail to the west coast of Scotland. It was built in 1933, but became the *Queen Mary II* when a bigger steam liner was constructed. It worked the Clyde during World War Two and retired after being fitted with oil burners in the 1970s. It was bought out by a distillery, restored, and is a pleasurable place to sup in the Thames air. You can sit on the upper deck and view the busy bus boats, the tourist boats, and sometimes wave at them. There's also the grand view of Waterloo Bridge down to Parliament and the London Eye.

I stopped and paused briefly to alleviate the lactic acid in my legs, giving them a good solid stretch. I took a glug or two of energy drink and to recoup from the run so far. I checked my watch. Good timing so far... wow, how fit am I? What is Johnnie missing with a body like mine! I patted my thighs and my neatly compressed tummy. Mind you, lifting patients about gives you strong core muscles. As does having to push Jenny's car to get it started every now and then when she is too lazy to take the tube in.

I don't know why she doesn't trade it in, what with the government's scrap age scheme. Sentimental value, she larks. Blimey, some people. Well, it was keeping me in shape.

I smiled to myself and stretched up skywards and thanked the gods for it not completely chucking down. My reprieve over, I rocketed on to the thump of Lenny Kravitz.

Cleopatra's Needle was swarmed by young little holiday makers climbing over the face of it. I wondered if they knew anything of its history, its real meaning. That it really is one of two ancient needles from the city of Heliopolis that were erected by Thutmose III around 1450 BC. Then they were moved to a temple in Alexandria in honour of Mark Anthony by Cleopatra. Then the pair of needles were toppled and buried some time later, and their faces of red granite were preserved under the sand. The London needle is twin of the New York City needle, but a Paris one has a different origin. It was presented to the British in 1819 by Mehemet Ali, the viceroy of Egypt, to commemorate the victories of Lord Nelson over the battle of the Nile. It didn't leave for London until 1877, as the transportation costs were too high and the needle's move needed to be sponsored. It was erected after a terrible journey and fear of loss at sea on 12 September 1878 on Victoria Embankment. You can still see some of the shrapnel wounds on it from World War I German planes in 1917 and their attempt at a first blitz on London.

I was then at the embankment station with more buses, cycle couriers, black cabs, odd cars, big businessmen's cars, Mercs, Jags, Porsches, and a Ferrari. His shades were rubbish and he was in the wrong gear. Ha, fabulous.

I was jogging along at a good pace towards Parliament. It

felt good; the light spring rain eased my tension and cleared my head. It was amusing to see the tourists out in their hustling buses, their cameras clicking away, their excited pointing, smiling at the local attractions. Then it was across Westminster Bridge, towards the South Bank and the London Eye.

It was amazing how the face of London redevelops and reinvents itself, reclaiming its mystery. My iPod blasted out a random mix of death rock, Frank Sinatra, Guns N' Roses, eighties hits, Jamiraquai, Bob Marley, Prince, Kylie, Michael Jackson, Jackson 5, Abba, Pink, some Coldplay too, and some other weird stuff that Simon downloaded for me. The pace was good and the tourists weren't too intensely crowded yet. I smiled to myself from time to time about the escapades of the previous night and about not having to be on the receiving end of someone being irritated and abusive in the A&E unit. Poor Simon was on duty I just hoped he did not have too bad a headache. I then hoped that Johnnie would be lying in some German cell for being rude and doing "heil Hitler" goose-stepping.

The London Eye was queuing already and the aquarium was slowly supporting the awaiting queue by opening its doors at last. Funny what they turn some of the older buildings into. Apparently there was a tube station beneath County Hall that was closed during the blitz for the MPs to use as a war cabinet. I think they filmed part of a Bond movie there also. I went up along Jubilee Walkway, dodging through the bustling crowd, through Jubilee Gardens to sound of Madness and The Prince. I was getting a good pace, but my legs were feeling tired. "Keep going," I thought loudly in my head, grunting while shoving some handle-barred German out of the way.

I ran past The Royal Festival Hall, the place never ceases to amaze me. It was built post-war, and some crazy enthusiast listed it as Grade I! It's like a chicken coop. It was opened in 3 May 1951. The foundation stone was laid by prime minister Clement Attlee in 1949. The building was built over the site of the Lion Brewery. I gave a small giggle at the thought of England hosting the Eurovision song contest there in 1960 hosted by Katie Boyle. The famous Hayward building was built in 1967 as part of the South Bank development. I stopped to straighten my lactic-acid filled muscles and sip on my energy drink. To be honest, a good coffee would have sufficed right then, with a mass of sugar and cream. Mmm.

With that thought, I chippered on up the walk. My scrunched up pony tail bobbed, sodden with fresh spring rain. The trees were still sleeping and there was no real sign of a pardon from winter, no fresh buds quite yet. A week or so and the whole bank would be bursting forward in new life as well as more of the enthused camera snappers.

Sometimes Simon and I played guess-the-nationality. Simon tended to win the most, as he is native to the area and has a sharp eye.

With so many things on the South Bank, it could get quite choked up in the summer months.

Ah, next was the Royal National Theatre. Well, it spoke for itself. Prince Charles is a keen fan and wonders at its construction; it's pretty ugly on the outside but has an amazing ergonomic use of all of the theatres and stages inside. You could see both Shakespeare and modern performances. It had been in developed over the 1960s and 1970s due to the requirement of financial backing. But it was opened on 22 October 1963 in the Olivier theatre with the performance of Hamlet. It was part of the RSC – the Royal Shakespeare Company – which was founded in Stratford-upon-Avon in 1879.

I ducked down towards bank's end, past the Anchor pub (built 1615), down the cobbles, careful not to turn an ankle, under the heavy railway bridge with Bar Blue on the right. The Bar stretched right back under the bridge, all glinting of glass and neatly placed cutlery. Waganama was opposite. I pondered for a moment about what the bridge would have been years back. Probably warehouses and storage. I smiled again to myself as I entered Clink Street. The Clink was a medieval prison from 1151 to 1780; it was voted London's worst prison. Hence, the terminology of putting you in the clink. I smelled the aroma of sweet coffee and Starbucks. I decided that temptation was too great and laiden did a fast walk back to King George House.

I retuned home with the daily newspaper, a Starbucks cappuccino, and a well-deserved bacon roll from the local market stall, which had already set up for Saturday trading at Borough Market. The market was great for fresh food stuffs, both the weird and wonderful. It's right under the railway and the clunking and clickty-clack rumble of trains echoed overhead in a soothing manner.

The concierge gave me a nod and a big grin as I trundled my tired body through the foyer. The apartments were on the upper levels and the lower floor was used for business, belonging to a guild now.

The London air was full of moisture and the promise of spring blossom. I supped in its vista from the front balcony, chomping my roll and slurping my coffee. I decided that I would shower, give Jenny a buzz, and do a bit of retail therapy.

I read the daily newspaper, with its usual celebrity tat on the front page, but it had an interesting article about World War II and the real Churchill. Apparently, he was a correspondent of the *Daily Mirror* paper prior to the war. Full of coffee and with aching legs and bacon rolling around my tum, I took in the information. I closed the paper and folded it neatly on the table. It was a habit of tidiness from the discipline instilled during my boarding-school days.

I had an odd sensation as I left the main room to shower. I felt as if I was being watched and there was the full stench of heavy tobacco. I was quite sure I saw something for a fleeting moment: the wafting of tobacco smoke, a hand holding a very large cigar. My mind raced, too much of the old ice-cream and self-sympathy booze from the night before. However, when I curiously crept back into the main living area, my newspaper was gone. A spine chill ran through me, and I coughed on the presence of the smoke and ash that had been carelessly flicked on the floor. I called out to see if there was a response; there was none, as I had expected. The door was bolted, the window was bolted, and I knew I was alone. I searched the entire apartment to no avail. Shaking my head, I assumed madness through stress.

We decided on Camden Town and King's Road; Oxford Street was always a drag, so busy with tourists not really buying but window shopping. A lot of them get caught up in how busy it really is, with all the shoving and huffing. It wasn't that way for me. I liked unusual items. For some reason, I have a fascination with rummaging in second-hand shops; it's amazing what you could find. I found some old military uniforms, and I got Simon a Russian jacket one time and the cool hat that matched with it. He wasn't too impressed in wearing something second-hand, but appreciated its true warmth.

Jenny and I bought some new tops, and I found an old vase perfect for my dinning table. I just needed flowers. Ah, but then there was the temptation of shoes. I bought some rather fab new DMs. They were bright red Doc Martens boots, perfect with some skinnies.

We popped in for lunch down from Covent Garden into the Princess of Wales, near Charing Cross on Villiers Street. Jenny had chicken tikka panini, and I tucked into a good old-fashioned ploughman's, with side of chips of course. After all, it was my birthday. We doused ourselves with a cheap bottle of plonk – although it really was a good value wine. Simon and some of the other guys from the hospital go on hunts for real ale, and this was one place they tormented on occasion.

Apparently the pub had hidden secrets of associations and secret marriages. You just needed to be careful going down into the toilets. Jenny slipped on her chunky boots and nearly went the whole way tumbling the dog-legged stairwell. So narrow and steep, that it could only pass one person at a time. It felt as if you would find the Thames at the foot of the stair well. Of course, we both fell about laughing and blocked the entire passage while frolicking about. Some poor, overweight middle-aged bloke got wedged at the foot because we couldn't contain our humour.

We apologise and explained our predicament and the chap chuckled at Jenny's folly.

We headed off home after traipsing around Covent Garden market and buying some new earrings and facial shrapnel for Jenny. She stood at one point considering another adornment attachment. I retorted by informing her that she would start leaking when she drinks if she had anymore. She scowled at my sarcastic comment. Jenny suggested that I stock up my wine cellar, thrusting a large note in my hand. She waited for her bus in the swirling drizzle and promised not to be late. It was getting dark.

I arrived back toKing George House, carrying bags full of new clothing, wine, and chocolate. It was not a big birthday, but somehow it felt that way. I relaxed in a well-deserved bath and hoped that I didn't nod off in it. It fizzed away with one of those lush bath bombs, one with those sparkles on it like fairy dust. Ah, it was so warm, a relief to my poor, run-out body. Perhaps I shouldn't have pushed myself so much earlier. Never mind, I figured I would feel the benefit of it later, and hopefully later in life. I smiled to myself contented with the knowledge of my fitness. I listened to the iPod on its mobile dock on the window sill. It was not really giving out a lot of noise but just enough volume for comfortable listening. I didn't know how much Simon has downloaded; he said it didn't take too long, as according to him you can fast download the tracks Me, I know little of such technology, being from Africa and all, I tell him. We laugh, stating that I would be good with a rock and chisel.

The water was deep and warming. It was not a good combination of a belly full of wine and sinking into such a relaxing mood, but my mind was washed of Johnnie and his hurtfulness. The music seemed to drift and fade.

I was gasping, choking. My face was sodden and eyes were sore and stinging. I felt something touch me. It touched my head and then grabbed my neck.

I couldn't open my eyes. I reached for the towel, but it was somehow given to me, placed in my hand. I rubbed my face furiously and let out a scream.

I was alone.

My eyes focused, and I swear I saw a man. Dark-haired with rolled-up shirt sleeves, braces, and a roll-up dangling from the lips. I leapt from the bath, splashing, spilling the luxurious water across the floor. I pulled the towel tight and close around me. I called out, "Hello." No answer. I called again, "Hello." No reply. I stumbled to the bathroom door, but it was still bolted – a habit from flat-sharing for years. A sudden shudder shot through my spine. I smelled Old Spice and tobacco. I turned sharply to look towards the window. Nothing, the window was tightly closed and the iPod was playing. It was now belting out Michael Jackson's "Thriller.". Pants – that all I needed. I then laughed very loudly; what a bizarre moment. To think someone was perving me in the starkers. Ha ha, I should have been so lucky. But the smell... I sat on the rim of the footed bathtub and hugged the towel, recomposed myself, and refocused on the night ahead. I wished I wasn't so near-sighted – I couldn't see the face clearly. Was it a ghost? My ghost?

Or was it my over-active imagination mixing with the wine and warm water?

I dried myself, put in a fresh pair of lenses, and prepared for a fab night out.

I actually put on my new top and skirt, wore a big flamboyant belt, and buckled up my ears with the new adornments from Covent Garden market. I twirled in front of the mirror and gave myself a big" looking good girl".

# THE EVENING OUT

Simon was a little late arriving at the flat; he had to be on call for an emergency at the ophthalmic department. He profusely apologised. He hovered in the doorway for a period of time, unlike him, and declined to enter. He had been spooked the previous night and didn't want that experience again. I didn't tell him about the bath – maybe later when his mind was more rested with a few jars of real ale in his tummy. He held a small present. He always remembered and was always generous. The present was a lovely little, delicate necklace with a golden cat dangling from it. He smiled, shuffling from one foot tot the other. "Well, I know you like them, and you can't have pets here, so it's also supposed to be lucky. Like a guardian. It's Chinese, of course," he rambled. "You do like it, don't you?"

"Of course I do, silly. I love all the different oddities. It's just very me. Thank you." I give him a kiss on his cheek and offered my neck for the new item to be strung. He proceeded to harp on about my little trick the previous night and stated that he was unsure about the supernatural and would get advice. I just laughed. He mentioned the aroma of maleness in the flat from where he stood. I denied any knowledge of it, although I could still smell that Old Spice since the bath incident. I shuddered and grinned at the thought of what had happened.

Jenny arrived refreshed and with the new placements of the day's purchases.

She groomed herself with a dash of gin in the kitchen. But I guess she really wanted to have a nose about of what Simon had told her. She paused in front of the mirror, threw heckling sounds at Simon, and picked up with a glass of chilled chardonnay, clunking down the empty gin glass.

I opened a bottle of wine and filled more glasses for the three of us. Simon paused back over to the doorway, supping his wine. He felt uncomfortable being in the room.

I finished of my wine. Then my eye caught Jenny touching the glass, and as she did so, she went pallid and screamed. She dropped her now-empty glass, as she had glugged it down while viewing the mirror, and shot past Simon, bellowing, "Ghost!"

I laughed a false kind of laugh to try and settle the pair of them. Simon started flapping his arms again. "Jesus, guys, you two are spooking me out. Is it a formula to get me to sell up?" I rebuked them both. Simon stopped flapping and Jenny stood quite still; she was shocked by something. I slowly paced back across the room and glanced in the mirror. I saw only myself and the contents of my flat. I laughed even louder. "You guys get the creeps about anything."

"Serious, I saw a man's face. He was, he was..." Jenny's words were staccato and her body was trembling.

"Go on," I encouraged her.

"He was... dancing... naked."

I roared with laughter. "Pity Simon didn't see him!"

That was it. Jenny folded her arms and stood in the doorway, defiant.

"We take you out, and all you can do is play practical jokes on us?"

"You try living with the aroma of Samson tobacco and Old Spice."

"What's wrong with Old Spice?" Simon retorted, giving a huge slurp.

"Nothing. It's kind of... nice." I paused, slurping back from the wine now.

"Let's get some sake down us," Jenny pleaded.

We left.

We first attended to Simon's needs and called in at the George Inn near the market. The old Tudor building had low ceilings and was a tourist attraction again. Jenny marched across the courtyard to the Heeltap bar for cocktails and came back out with my cousin, Stephan and his mates Paul, Raj, Jay, and Johan. We sat under the gas heaters in the courtyard, as not to offend either clientele buying from each premises. It was kind of cosy and the warm glow of the lamps and heaters set up a friendly face against the drizzly dark evening. We were going on to meet a whole tribe across the river in Soho. We all marched across London Bridge, arm in arm, singing. Stephan and I recalled some old South African melodies and just to hack the others off, we clacked away in Afrikaans.

Stephan was like a big brother to me. Not quite as cool as Uncle. He handed me A large, handwritten envelope, addressed in full. I knew who the envelope was from – Uncle.

He always remembered too and was always generous. The contents I knew full well would pay for the evening's extravaganza. Stephan gave me a wink, whispered to me, "Little sis," and pecked me on the cheek. Simon picked up on it and confirmed his jealousy by announcing that that sort of thing shouldn't go in families. We all laughed. Jenny didn't like walking and complained her feet were hurting and her hair was getting bedraggled. Paul offered his umbrella and bravely took her by the arm, escorting her through the elements across the bridge. Simon kept his eye firmly fixed on Stephan, as if he had a chance.

We marched up past Monument and gave in to the elements as the rain came down harder, and we mounted the bus to Soho. It was a short stop away, but the traffic was heavy, and it took some while to reach our destination. We annoyed the other passengers with our renditions of Stevie Wonder's "Happy Birthday" with the accompaniment on my portable iPod speakers. The bus driver smiled for a change at our cheery mood. We had been thrown off before at Christmas for making a din!

I am not a particular fan of Chinese food, but I enjoyed the massive atmosphere of Soho – Leicester Square, the lost tourists, the buzz of the Irish bar. Yes, the Irish bar with its live music. We met the rest of the troops in the bar, and we couldn't hold back Diane from the open mike. We had tears rolling down our faces as the patrons' ears bled.

Wow, what a fantastic party.

The best birthday ever and there was no slime bag to poise on my shoulder. However, I did fall asleep, much to the amusement of my friends in the middle of the la Fumarar

# THE MIRROR

restaurant. I missed the chopstick fight and the dressing up of my hair with chopsticks and carnations.

It was getting a cab back that I really couldn't recall. The cabbies almost declined our fare, but Stephan persuaded him to take us with a large wedge of cash up front.

Diane from orthopaedics was a real brick by giving me a hand up the stairs and plonking me inside the door. The odd thing was everyone else refused to enter the premises. They dumped me down, kissed and hugged me goodnight, and suggested that they call it a night at 2:00 a.m.

I thanked them a thousand times for a wonderful evening.

The problem is when you've had too many drinks, you end up going past all reasoning and, of course, you get the insatiable appetite for bacon sandwiches or kebabs. Well, you can imagine the condition I was in. However, on the third attempt at opening the fridge, I found the bacon. Pouring myself a large glass of Lindeman's chardonnay to toast the success of a fab evening, I ignited the grill, plonking the strips of bacon under it. I do not recall anything else.

# THE INCARNATION

She slipped; falling against the side unit, banging her head, landing on the wine glass and slashing open her hand. It was not long before the grill caught fire, smouldering the bacon, billowing smoke around the kitchen. The smoke alarms set off their intense sirens. However, she didn't wake. Lucky for her, her friends had not managed to catch a taxi (despite requesting the driver to wait, he had gone into the night) They were still hovering in the stairwell of the flats, waiting for the rain to ease. Simon flew back up the stairs, banging on the door, calling her name. There was no response. He remembered that there was a hidden key in the hallway just in case she locked herself out. The concierge had gone for the night, but there was the duty security officer.

Fast on his feet, he and the guard searched for the key.

Samantha's friend Diane banged hard on the door. A neighbour rose from his slumber, inquiring what the commotion was about. He too banged hard on her door. Simon found the key — it was hidden in the terracotta pots in the foyer, and he burst through the heavy oak door. There was no smoke. He shot across to the living room and froze. Samantha was lying on the sofa, stretched out with her hand being bandaged up by a naked man. Not just any naked man, but it was the face he had seen in the mirror the day before. Just as their eyes met, the naked man vanished, like a magician without the puff of smoke. Stunned momentarily, Simon leapt across the room to seek out the stranger. He was nowhere to be seen. Diane brushed past the scowling Simon and attended to Samantha. The guard enquired if all was okay and left, chastising them and requesting the electrics and alarms be rechecked.

Diane went into the bathroom for smelling salts. She knew Samantha kept a lot of her med stuff in the cabinet in there and there were always salts. She froze, an eerie creeping sensation trickled down her spine and the scent of Old Spice almost over whelming her. She darted sharply from the room with the bottle and aroused Samantha with the salts. They proceeded to enquire what had happened. Samantha didn't remember. Simon checked the kitchen. There was a broken glass, neatly swept up; the grill had been lit but had been extinguished with a damp tea towel. The window had been opened to let out the smoke.

Diane inspected the girl's hand. She unravelled the neatly wound bandage. It was thick, heavy wadding she hadn't seen for many years, but it was neat, clean, and tidy. The wound had been stitched neatly with tiny, delicate, and accurate sutures, neatly packed to protect it. Simon and Diane looked at each other with puzzlement. Samantha knew nothing of the naked man. Simon blew out his cheeks in wonderment. He shrugged his shoulders and, being a little too intoxicated to explain anything to A&E, made an amicable decision to leave the girl tucked up in bed. He volunteered to stay the night with Samantha. He did, however, leave her in the living room and slept in her bed. He found the presence of the mirror too spooky, although he covered it with a sheet he found under the bed. He wrapped himself in a large bathroom towel, placing the duvet over the intoxicated, frail-looking girl. He didn't really care where he slept, however, but he found the whole thing disturbing.

He wondered if he was losing his marbles and pondered if something had been dropped in his drink by Johan. His thoughts though were of Stephan, and his nostrils filled with Old Spice.

# THE WOODEN BOX

The day after my birthday, I awoke to find myself with a large hangover headache, my hand tightly bandaged up, and I was on my sofa. Simon was attending to me, fetching and carrying things from the kitchen; he looked shattered, a ghost of himself. I enquired about what had happened the previous night. He just shrugged his shoulders in a manner saying "I do not do mornings." I was informed we were going to visit A&E and to have a session with the local fire brigade on safety in the home. I was puzzled by his demands and requested a further explanation.

He told me to ask the mirror. "Mirror, mirror on the wall, what do we need from you at all?" Simon sneered at it. I noticed it was covered by one my under sheets.

I dangled my hand down onto the carpet and touched a small wooden box. I reached and clasped it, holding it to get a better feel of its texture. I slowly lifted it so I could view it better. Somehow, I managed to remove my contact lenses the night before; I couldn't recall doing it. Simon was still prattling in the kitchen. I asked him whilst lifting the small box what happened to my hand. He made noises of reprimand at me. I persisted at his reprimand, and he rebuked my drunken folly. Anyone would have thought that Simon was my mother. Well, I guess he had been the closest thing to it over the past few years.

I clutched the box, tilting it to focus my blurry eyes on the inscription. Across the top of the box in an old form of etching were the words "Charles Hamilton Smythe". I felt the wooden texture. I found the catch to open it. Pop. I lifted open the lid wearily and looked at its contents. I gasped at the contents. Simon heard my gasping and rushed in like a nursemaid. I peered up into his eyes and enquired where the box originated. He started that flapping of his arms again, glaring at the mirror. I requested he removes the cover from it. He profoundly refused and started yammering on about a naked man being in my apartment. At that point, my head was the size of the Gherkin Tower, and I lost it, yelling him to stop being a melodramatic queen.

That didn't help. But he insisted that at the hospital they could assess my hand better, along with my mind and his crazy brain. Perhaps there was a $CO_2$ leak making us go bananas and hallucinate. He told me to make myself presentable. In other words, to get my ass into gear and clean up so he could end his stint as nursemaid.

My uncle was senior consultant at the hospital. He was a cool, stony-faced man that struck your heart as being no-nonsense strict, but he was not a tyrant. His heart was deep within, so some folks felt he was unkind with his straight-talking words. Great, all I needed was a lecture on how binge drinking was dangerous to the health and safety. Perhaps I could be a case study for his students. Pah, they were all out getting lashed up to the point of George Best syndrome. However, I was not afraid of him; he spoke many truths and had been fair to both me and Stephan throughout our lives.

We left two and a half hours later when my stomach could face the world.

We reached A&E and one of my old colleagues recognises me and, of course Simon – everyone remembers Simon!

We were taken through to one of the nurses' stations and asked to wait. Shit, my uncle was on duty!

Simon sat fiddling with the blinds and tutting that the bags hadn't been emptied and that they should have been done before the dayshift. If he had been in charge of the unit, heads would have rolled. He suggested we not touch anything, especially if Fraulien Gerbels was about. He hated Gerbels; her real name, Sister Hemlock, says it all really.

Uncle appeared from behind the curtain, coughed lowly to clear his throat and to let us know he was there. Gerbels had gone and got him!

He approached me, smiling in that condescending manner that made Simon switch from one crossed-leg position to another. My uncle flicked his finger against his chin in the cool manner of his.

"Well, what have we here?" he said, smirking at my predicament. "Too much drink at the weekend? You know how I feel about excess drinking. It's a real big problem in this country now. A&E is full of idiots on a Saturday night that I have to put back together." He sat down on the chair next to me. I twitched, hoping that Gerbels would leave before the full launch of his torrid preaching.

"Let me see," he reached out an open hand to me, offering me to submit the injured hand.

He gently unwound the heavy bandages, inspecting them with curiosity. The wadding came away to reveal the neatly stitched wound. He gasped at the precise formation of the stitches. Looking up into my eyes, he enquired about who had performed the surgical procedure. I looked nervously at Simon, who was squirming. Simon gazed down to the floor, then gave me a disapproving sideways glance.

"Who did this?" uncle pushed with puzzled expression, scowling. Simon flicked his fingers across his chin and then rubbed one of his eyes, trying to hide his discomfort. I shrugged my shoulders. I glanced up at Simon's face, searching for help. Simon was sheepishly observing the floor and Uncle's shoelaces. I remembered the wooden box and the carvings on it in my bag, shooting a glance at the bag. Uncle glanced to the bag and then enquired about it. Simon crossed and uncrossed his legs in agitation. Simon surrendered to participated in the moment and passed over the bag, opened it, and reluctantly handed over the small wooden box.

Uncle gasped. "Where on Earth did you get this?" He scratched his head, having released my hand. Again I shrugged my shoulders and searched Simon's face for a little support. He still glanced down like some reprimanded child, almost sulking.

Uncle glared at Simon, and Simon lifted his head to the steely eyes. He then sprung to his feet and did that flapping-arm thing he did and started blurting, "It was the ghost. It was the ghost!"

Uncle lost his patience and boomed at him to get a grip and remain seated.

## THE MIRROR

He held the box and gently undid the small brass catch. He let out an astonished gasp, and a small twinkle appeared in his eyes. It unsettled me. Uncle was one of the shrewdest, strictest professionals, who left his staff trembling when he disciplined another on the ward.

"Well, well," he smiled, shaking his head, forgetting about the sorry state my hangover was in and how my hand was. Uncle then gently toyed with the box's contents. "A kit for field surgeons in World War II, neatly packaged and finely preserved. A real treasure." He respectfully closed the small wooden box and observed the name upon it. "Wow, a real treasure trove." He paused and then glimpsed briefly away from the box, up into my eyes. "Where did you get it again?"

Simon was twitchy again.

I answered honestly, "I found it in my flat." I can see Simon was getting his arms ready for takeoff. Uncle scowled disapprovingly. He glanced from Simon back to me and back to Simon and then back down to the box.

"Very well," he announced. "Take good care of it."

"Who is he?" I enquired with interest in his response. He laughed and then scowled back at me.

"My dear, you don't study the hospital's history enough." And with that, he got up and strode to leave. But he got one more pop at me. "Stay off the drink, and keep that handiwork clean. Come see me in a week to have those stitches removed." He strode back out of the little rest area, shaking his head in puzzlement. I gasped at Simon. What the hell was all that about? He shrugged his shoulders and then did that little arm flap and announced he wasn't hanging around my flat anymore. I sat perplexed about the little wooden box.

I ran my finger across the name engraving: Charles Hamilton Smythe. Who was this person, and who was the ghost in the mirror? My mirror. It seemed everyone else had a good look at him except me. Simon announced he was leaving me in the capable hands of Hemlock Gerbels to re-bandage my hand and flounced off, twittering about the cruelness of the world and his headache. Gerbels enjoyed the reprimand and informed me that I could only do desk work for the duration of the healing process because of infections and all that. Especially with my medical history. What a bitch, I think, just because I had malaria all those years ago, and a form of hepatitis.

# STEPHAN

Stephan met me at the hospital gates, his eyes red and blurry from the night before. He chuckled about me dozing off and threatened to publish me being dressing up over the Internet chat sites. "Oh, such a tease," I spit at him in Afrikaans.

He offered to buy me lunch and walked me up to the Anchor on Bank End. They do great Sunday roast. He enquires where Simon is and I shrug, "Somewhere else, most of the time. I think he had a gutful from Uncle and needed some brain-charging time."

Stephan apologised that Great-granddad was too unwell to come and that the Gestapo of a warden would not allow such an elderly gent out in such damp weather. Great-granddad was, of course, despondent to the demands and had to remained in custody of the warden. Perhaps we could go the next week to see him, when his cough had cleared. Stephan gave me a small card from him, handwritten in shaky quill ink. Lots of kisses and a small note was folded for a drink on him.

Stephan ordered me a real ale and announced it would

settle the tummy. We chatted about his ventures across Europe and how much he missed Alenka in Moscow. He hoped she could come to London and was trying to get her a work permit through the hospital. No chance for Simon, though, he was a dead-straight guy. He tells me how Alenka's grandparents fled the Germans from occupied Poland and snuck into Russia hidden in straw carts, savaging the land before the hard winters settled. They were befriended by a kind farming family and taught, kept, and worked hard. He told me how they were driven back further and further into the heart of Russia as Stalin burned towns, fields, and villages to disable the advance of the German invasion.

Stephan's eyes glazed over. "Such wonderful people. The people, so beautiful. The land was so hard and cruel. We hear of South Africa now, but the hardship continues there under cloak and dagger." He sighs.

"What's the next language you're learning?"

"Oh," his mind back on me again, "I thought about Japanese." He smiled, gazing around at the swell of tourists. "Tokyo is supposed to be a crazy man's dream," he laughed. "Gotta go try that."

"How long you in England for?" again I enquired.

"The post at the RNIB is for a three month contract, translating and assisting in new technologies." He shrugged. "Me dad won't employ me. For some reason he says I must make it myself as a man. Christ, how old does he think I need to be before he recognises I am not fifteen years old anymore."

I gently squeezed Stephan s hand with my wounded hand.

"I know," I sympathised. "He is just the same with me.

But a little more over–protective." Stephan gazed up from his half-devoured Yorkshire pudding and beef.

"He has reason to protect you." He smiles. "Remember, he swore an oath to look after you as well..." He trailed off, shuffling in his seat. "Anyway, birthday girl, what's this about your apartment being haunted?" Then he laughed. I laughed louder than he. And then the patrons were giving that shun look for being rowdy.

After we finished chomping, we set off for a walk down the South Bank in the drizzling rain again. How I missed the African sun at times.

He tormented me for a few moments about the haunted flat.

"Whotold you?" I insisted.

His eyes told me. "Jenny. That girl can't hold her tongue." I then blushed.

"Sorry about Simon and his roving eyes."

"Sorry? What for?" He laughed. "I am not a well-travelled man for no reason. I find it quite flattering!" He smirked and gave me a big dig in the ribs. "'Course you want to go to some of the cities I have been too. Sort you out an education, it would." His dirty laugh rattled against the cool Thames breeze.

I laughed back and called him a dirty-minded bastard. And no wonder his father is always pressuring him. He gave me a wink-wink, nudge-nudge. "Mmm," he started, "did I tell you about our boys' weekend in Amsterdam the other month? That was on our way from Moscow?"

"No," I replied wryly. "I really don't think it is for my pretty innocent ears, Stephan," I rebuked in a curtly, true manner. I think, "Boys and their dangly bits again,"

# THE OTHER ROOM

I got home a lot later than I assumed and headed for the chill cabinet and opened my old favourite of Lindemans chardonnay. My head was sore and in need of the hair of the dog that bit me. Still, it was difficult twisting out the cork with a rather sore hand. I wandered to the kitchen for a glass, viewing the burnt remnants of the bacon. I poised the now-full glass to my lips. Christ, everyone knew hospital staff were pushed to the limit and some require a wee tipple at the end of the day.

Oh well, I figured to hell with it. I was lucky to be in one piece; I blamed the sleazebag for all the problems I had and took a huge gulp from the glass. The really weird thing was I could smell that tobacco and rich aftershave aroma again. I was seriously going nuts. Perhaps I should attend the mental health unit in the morning. Hell no. There was nothing wrong with me, I was just a bit stressed out.

I crossed the living room, shunning my eyes from the mirror. I leaned out on the balcony and supped in the rich carbon dioxide air. That night, it smelt of wood burning from the barges. Barges? That night? I looked again and

# THE MIRROR

saw the river full of boats of all sorts: heavily laden barges, small tugboats, and a frigate ship. The river was very busy. What the hell were they burning? It seemed one or two or more were steam-driven. I squinted my eyes to clear my vision. I turned my head back towards the living room. All seemed clear there. I looked back to the river and gasped. Was I going bananas? The river was clear; it was a dull afternoon, apart from the small river police boat zooming up the centre and the tourist bus boats moored at the bank. I felt a chill run up my spine and strode back inside, catching my reflection in the mirror.

There in the mirror, I saw three men, no, four, sitting down around a small table. The chesterfield had moved and the fireplace was clearly alight with crackling wood. There was a short-legged table placed in front of the fire, with stools spaced evenly for the players.

I paused, startled by the image. It was my room but was overlayed by the images of the other furniture that I saw the other night. But this time the figures seemed distracted by what was happening around the table. Wow. I thought they might be playing poker. What the hell was I doing entertaining a haunting? I was fixed to the spot and watched the men intensely. I recognised one of the uniforms one of the men was wearing. He was playing a shrewd game; I could just work out his cards. He was a naval officer, high-ranking by if my history knowledge serves me right. One was very obviously army-based; the other I did not know.

I stared, watching the game. I supped from my glass, and the face, his face, looked up from across the room. I felt awkward at my spying. But he grinned cheekily and winked at me. In response, I raised my glass back and laughed. That was so stupid. The others did not notice the gestures, so I stayed there staring. I squinted my eyes to focus on the shrewd naval officer's cards. Christ, what a sad, lonely bastard I had become. Playing cards or cheating for something that is probably closely related to schizophrenia. I didn't care. I laughed and waved the numbers of the cards at the cheeky-faced ghost. He puffed strongly on his roll ups and winked at me through the fog. I supped my glass and waved a cheers and good luck, blowing him a kiss out of fun. I returned to the balcony to assure myself I was not completely mad. The Thames was as it should be. I briskly walked back by the mirror, but didn't look in. I dared myself not too. I stood in the kitchen and observed the cleanliness of it. Where the hell did the burnt bacon go?

I finished down the bottle and heard my uncle's words of advice about alcohol abuse. I took refuge in a hot, steamy bath with one of those amazingly zingy balls from Lush with all those rose petals and sparkly bits. However, I had to wrap my hand up in a poly bag.

Ah, bliss.

# THE DIARY

I get an early night and decide tomorrow to investigate the hospital in search of the owner of the wooden box.

Mary, the hospital curator, questions my curiosity into the matter of the history. I respond by explaining the reprimand of my uncle. I am given permission to enter the library. I seek out past surgeons and doctors in the library's info. There he is. My heart races.

He is a wartime surgeon, a physician in reconstructive work on limbs, digital, and facial characteristics. Amazing. I pull him up on the screen and nearly scream when I see the image of a faded sepia photograph. I cup my hands across my mouth in astonishment.

It is the ghost.

I catch my breath, my heart thumping hard.

I enquire if there are any records or notes of his. The system throws up a notebook, teaching records, surgical records, and, most intriguingly, a diary. I rise from my seat and ask the clerk if it is possible to view the item. She nods and enquired if I want the original or a copy. I ask for both, as I guessed I would not be able to take home the original.

She is gone for a few moments and my heart lurches in anticipation. As I am waiting, Jenny appears in the doorway of the library, beckoning me with one finger. She has a serious, strange look. I obey, twitching over my shoulder to see if the assistant has missed me. She must be down in the vaults. Jenny's face is somewhat pallid. I ask why she was feeling so. She replies, "I know someone who can clean your flat." Her voice is soft and trembling.

"You saying I'm dirty?" I retort at the remark.

Jenny sighs. "No, stupid. The ghost!"

I am astounded. "I don't dabble in that bullshit," I defend.

"Jesus, Samantha, when are going to face the fact that you've got uninvited guests!"

"Maybe I like my guest." Yes, I did enjoy the company. It was fun and now someone wanted to push it into the recycling bin. "I am happy, thank you." I spoke softly, as Jenny is a sensitive soul. She thinks she is as hard as nails. She looks it.

A voice calls me from behind. It's the assistant with my books. I bid Jenny farewell, but her voice is shrewd and determined. "I will be at your place Thursday with the help you need."

"Yeah, whatever, spooky," I taunt.

I take the books from the assistant and request a small, quite, discreet place to read.

I finger the leather-bound diary, and it has the same inscription on it as the wooden box. It is old and tatty with age. It smells musty but also of deep tobacco, the type I

# THE MIRROR

can smell in my flat. My skin flinches. The assistant stares at me and begins to speak with a forked tongue, "Why are you interested in that two-faced Nazi bastard?"

"I beg your pardon?" I retort, almost speechless. This woman is probably old enough to be my late mother's great aunt. The woman's mouth is tight at the edges from years of shushing or pipe smoking.

"He was a Nazi spy. Disappeared during the war. Not a trace of him anywhere. Left like those god damned doodle bugs. Buzz, buzz and, bang, kaboom."

"You sound like you knew him."

She twitches, her mouth tightens, hiding the answer to my question.

"What did he do that was so bad?"

"People went missing, according to the archives." She pauses. "A bit of a nut, with all that experimentation." She circles her index finger at her temple. "Go ahead, have a good laugh. Kill yourself."

"I thought he was a pioneering surgeon?" I quiz, waving my hand at the computer. "According to the archives, that is."

She nods and says, "Aye, he was." A small Scottish whisper of honesty. "I'll leave you in peace." She shuttles off in a kind of melancholy swagger.

I stare down at the diary. I am unsure if I should open it, but I feel more resolve to find out about the stranger I have wondering around my place.

I open the cover:

>   Diary of Charles Hamilton Smythe.
>   Mbq esq. surgeon of the Royal Hospital and

> professor of new science and technology
> development. 1941.
> Address: Apartment 4, King George House,
> Riverside Mead, London Bridge

I stare, mouth open. That's my address. My home. It makes sense. My heart races. I turn over the page:

> Blood type: O negative. Inoculations for all
> commanding officers and medical team up
> to date, last checked December 1940 for
> field combat situations.

There is also a note to himself:

> No such next of kin, except for the distant
> aunt in Australia. Can be contacted through
> the Royal London Infirmary of his Majesty,
> King George. God save the King and all of
> us from the devastating atrocities of war.

I feel this is not the writing of some mad Nazi spy. But how the hell do I know? They were a very clever race of hard thinkers. I turn over the cover page and begin to read. It is somewhat dull: clinical details from an early January about reconstructing tissues and the possibility of being able to grow cells for burn victims. I sigh; they have been doing that for years now. I pause and then read the procedure again. It's a basic format like all cell engineering. But was it possible then? Jesus, they were playing around with genetics and the Aryan race. I pause a while to absorb the man's brilliance and my complete misinterpretation of the script. I then shudder with the though that he probably was a Nazi, with all that superior intellect. But hang on a minute. Why couldn't one of our guys have been so brilliant? And why was old Mackey Fields so twitchy about this guy?

I read further into the diary with keen interest in the procedures. It was not much of a diary. Then it hit me whilst Mackey's wee mouth calls out that it's time for the library to close.

> March 4, 1941: Today is my well-earned rest and birthday. I sat tuned to the wireless, listening to the wretched war correspondence and heaving my heart over the many reconstructions I would be performing here in London over the next few days. I then smelt the heavy scent of what was probably a lady's cologne, it was floral. I smelt the scotch, but it was not the type that my good old friend Kyle J. C. Mckilloch had posted to me from Aberdeen. No mistaking it, it was a scent to make any man's head turn. For a moment, I assumed a trauma to my self from all the hard days and nights of welding soldiers and citizens together just for them to go out and be re-blown-up and land on the white table again for me to fix like some kind of surgical miracle. Yes, floral. A heavy scent that was intoxicating. I paced around the room to see if one of my overzealous students had

played some daft joke on me. Alas, no. I was holding the glass of scotch, a good source from the Tweed Valley, and then I froze, peering into my art deco mirror (that damned thing cost me a small man's ransom). Her hair was flowing like liquid rose petals. Beautiful. I was transfixed.

"Miss! We are closing now! Some of us have homes and wee families!"

I am yanked up into her glaring snarl that seemed to want to snap shut the book.

"Can I take it home?" Damn, I want to tell her to piss off. But it doesn't always work. Sometimes you have to keep the old trap shut.

She scowls a no, but she agrees that if my obsession is such, then I can take the printed copy but not the original. We agree.

It was the fastest journey home I ever had.

I get through my flat door and throw my keys and coat down. I toss the book down on the sofa and glimpse up at the mirror. I open the book.

The pages are overtyped! They seemed fine in the library. I flick furiously from page to page. Nothing. All double squiggled. I am furious. Mackey will have a wee piece of me mind in the morn. Cool joke on the girl obsessed with the psychotic maniac Nazi!

I lie in bed that night clasping the book and check every now and again to see if the pages are clean. Nothing. I fall into slumber a lot later than I want.

# THE COFFEE SHOP

I wake late. It is usually my early shift, and I get a phone call from the Sister telling me what a pain in the arse I am for smashing myself up over the weekend. But she ends the dialogue with, "Get well fast because we need you and the temp is crap."

I feel bad. My head is worse today. I am topped from yesterday. I look at the copy of the book and say to it that it's a piece of shit. Still, I hang onto it and carry it with me to down to the Starbucks opposite the hospital on the corner of Joiners Street and wait for the library to open. I order my usual and sit outside freezing my butt in the March rain. The thing is, in London you boil your brains out on the tube and get sweaty walking around the shops, so you travel with minimal clothing so as not to have those huge sweat rings hanging under your arms.

So I sat my butt down on one those cheese-grater type fashionable chairs. I have thought many times that they should have had one in the bloody Tower of London. Oh yes, I think, I can see it next to the rack. Modern torture by commercialism.

I try reading the book again over a frothy cappuccino that has dribbles of light rain flecking the head. I gasp. The text is fine. I read the preface. It was published in 1985 by some mad London company. I want to know who did it. And why. Mind you, there are all sorts of crazy folks here.

I read further. An old janitor discovered the book in the archives of medical journals. It was published in 1985 to commemorate fifty years since the Blitz. It's about a doctor on the edge of madness or suicide. Was he a spy? A Nazi? Or were people plain ignorant?

There are many questions in the preface, wondering if war is the true way to resolve oppression and if genetic formation is a way to improve us as individuals or as human beings. The book is more an autobiography than a copy of his actual notes.

I sip the coffee and end up with froth on my lip. As I place the cup down, I hear a familiar voice. I am stunned. Johnnie!

Of all the places to find me, he found me here in my own safe haven.

I immediately stand on my feet, clutching the book.

"What the hell are you doing here? You cheating liar!" I raise my coffee, and, before I know it, it's splashed on his deep-suede coat.

"You bitch," he retorts, lunging for me. But I am too quick. I drop the book. I grab it with my good hand, but he catches my injured hand. He grips it tightly, squeezing it to increase the pain. I twist under his strain. Then he releases it as fast as it was grasped. I breathe heavily, panting in bewilderment. I clasp the hand in shock of the pain. A young man reaches to attend me. I refuse and stand upright to see Johnnie knocked off his feet, out cold on the concrete pavement with his head wedged between two chairs.

The manager from the coffee shop rushes out and the young guy starts to explain. I hear, but I do not listen. A police officer is called from across the road at the hospital gates, and an inquisition is performed. The young man denies slamming Johnnie to the floor, but says a passer-by seemed to recognise me and gave him a real right hook. But then he vanished as fast he was on the scene. I am asked to give a statement and also asked by the coffee shop owner not to return, at least for a while. WPC Lindsey Gillingham races towards the scene. I know her very well. She is an old friend from back when I first came back to England. She used to do my home studies for me just to give me some peace from my aunt. We would then go and guzzle down cider in her dad's garage, and she even got weed from time to time. She lost her mum to cancer when she was eleven, and although she is extremely intelligent, she was a full-out rebel.

The scene is cleared as Johnnie is taken into custody for assaulting me. The young man at the table next to me gives witness to it.

A dazed Johnnie is plonked in the back of a patrol car, his lip bleeding and face swelling.

I am left standing with the drizzle sticking my hair against my face like a limp lettuce leaf we leave in the fridge for four weeks just to keep the mind guilt free of all that junk crap we endlessly stuff in our faces.

I turn to ask the young man about my rescuer, but he shrugs his shoulders and says, "Could have been my dad by the way he smelt and with his hair." He laughs. "Fucking good right hook, though. Who was that prat squeezing your hand?"

I stare at him for a moment and reply indignantly, "Some scumbag I knew."

The policeman is taking down a statement from the coffee shop owner and WPC Gillingham takes mine, winking at me. "That was probably not the best thing to have done, miss. I know he banged into you, knocking your drink over, I saw it happen from across the road." She smiles. "Was that real suede? Bit passé, isn't it?" She informs me they will be in touch and that if I know of anything about the right-hook-giver to let them know. There could be charges on both sides for assault.

She winks with a wry smile, that smile that I know all too well. "Who was the gent, miss," she enquires. "Quite a looker, and a good right hook, I'd say." She continues, "Looked foreign to me. We may want to ask him for a statement, what with Mr Fenny having a broken jaw by the looks of it." She pauses at my pallid face. "You all right?"

My hand is sore. Not just sore, but banging with pain. It's so bad I feel my senses lessening. I can't stand much longer.

I don't quite hear her. Everything is fading to a brown colour. My butt hits the floor, and I murmur. WPC Gillingham springs forwards to assist me.

"You all right, missy?" I can't respond because the pain is so intense. I guess that the bastard has broken several bones with that crushing grip. I peer through my blurred vision to look at the seeping, blooded bandages.

"You need doctor, miss"

I shake my head. I couldn't go to the nearest A&E

– Uncle. I hear a voice behind me. I am pulled up by a tall, dark-haired man who informs the WPC he will take me to the infirmary.

An argument fires up between them. WPC Gillingham wants a statement, but the man is pulling me away from the scene. The police car with Johnnie in has now gone and only the two officers are left at the scene.

"Excuse me," I whisper, "it's okay guys. St Thomas college hospital. Better hurry, I can't take much more. I kind of laugh in hysterics. "Ha, without puking!"

The man puts his arm around me. I don't care; he seems familiar, safe.

They nod in agreement. Gillingham gives permission, but insists the doctor comes back to the station later to give a statement.

We stagger across the road, away from the heavy thunder of the construction traffic and machinery.

I notice how tall this guy is and how strong. He takes me in through the old courtyard and there are some strange smells and motorcars – motorbikes old, ancient, oily – parked up in the front court.

# THE HOSPITAL

The hospital smells different, of iodine. The corridors are displaced. My head hurts; I feel my legs wobble. The man grips me, keeps me from falling. Urgent words are called. An attending nurse comes. I gasp. The uniform, the hair. Then I know nothing. I pass out.

I awake several times, dozy, disorientated. I am in bed. Bedpans are fetched and carried. I am required to use them and not to make a nuisance of myself again by arguing to use the flushing toilet. My hand is wrapped up and strapped to a drip trolley. It hurts, but my fingers are straight and I can feel them. I am force-fed soups and potatoes and then sedated again to relive the pain and to make me more comfortable. I believe I am dreaming. I believe on occasion the tall man visits me. He sits quietly watching, observing, checking my hand and vitals. He pokes a thermometer in my mouth and smiles gently, taking my pulse. I cannot see too well. I was wearing my eyeglasses when Johnnie attacked me; somehow they are lost. I cannot see without them. I ask the tall man if he has seen them. He shakes his head but then mentions they are probably at the shop, as he recalls something fell from my head when Johnnie twisted my hand. Pants, I can't see, but I can smell and hear acutely. He smells of... no... the tobacco and that aftershave, but with a slight hint of iodine. I speak low and enquire his name. He admits his first name is Charles. There's a loud noise, a wailing from outside, a loud thundering discord. He injects me. I am unable to care about the fracas now and drift in and out of blissful consciousness. I remember the ward was basic, primitive in attire and instrumentations. I wonder where my bag was.

It was probably early morning when I awoke fully focused. I was in familiar surroundings. Not where I want to be, though. I am in an A&E bed with Simon flapping over me.

"What happened," I quiz. Beckoning him to come closer as I was unable to see him clearly due to my myopia.

"I called at your home, and..." he stammered, "you weren't there. I heard about that bastard at the coffee shop, and I spoke to WPC Gillingham at the station." He continued to ramble and flap. "It was all very worrying, and then..." I urged him to get to the point of what the hell I was doing in A&E. "Well, staff nurse Jones – you know the one, the big, fat, hairy-lipped thing that terrifies me, well, she found you."

"Where, Simon?" I barked at him. "I have a piece missing up here. That is why I am asking you." I was agitated.

He looked hurt at my demand, and I gave him a sad, doe-eyed sorry to get him to continue.

"She found you in the old part of the hospital... in a bed ... with a drip... and your hand all fixed up with some ancient bandages and a set of x-rays that look like they have been done on something out of Noah's ark. Your bag was stashed under the bed."

"What? Where in the hospital and what the hell is up with me? And I can't see."

"Uncle, your uncle is pressing charges against Johnnie because of the damage and there was a witness to what he did." He began to speed up with his explanation to the point where it began to blur. "Well, according to the previous visits and scans on your hand when you-know-what happened..."

"Yes, Simon, go on."

"He burst three of the small blood vessels. He Ripped the ligaments, causing misalignment and probable permanent disability." I knew he had something else to say. "But it's not all bad. Well, odd, really. They x-rayed you again and scanned your hand and found that you were in the hospital, well, two days ago exactly."

"What? I have lost two days?" he nodded.

"You were still quite heavily sedated and, well, the police will need to speak to you and Uncle, and it's all very strange."

"Simon, what's happened to me?"

"Well, someone has fixed it, basically." He shrugs his shoulders. "A good job, actually. Erm, probably better than anyone could do here except for Dr Omar, but he is in Egypt. And that doesn't explain anything. The healing process is far too advanced for a two-days absence. It's just bizarre."

"So you're telling me someone operated on my hand and dumped me in the hospital's ancient wing? Is that what you're telling me?"

He kind of nods, but continues, "Not exactly 'dumped.' You were in good condition and had all those strange medical files with you and some written explanation of what had been done."

"Show me."

"Can't." He shrugs his shoulders. "Uncle has them." Shit, I think I could have recognised the hand writing.

"So when can I leave?"

"Better ask hairy lip." He nervously twitches. I hear footsteps pacing up behind him. I instantly know them and hold my breath.

"Care to explain?" the voice rumbles.

Simon flaps and stands aside.

"Seems to be a real mystery about you lately, young lady. Care to shed some light on what is going on? The police are involved now, and I will make sure that idiot gets slammed away for the way he treated you." He glares at Simon to leave. He does but gives a flick of his wrist in disgust, the way he does when he gets bemused.

I start by explaining to Uncle the incident in the coffee shop and then the hospital. Yes, the uniform. I explain everything that I can possibly remember. glimpsing down at my padded hand.

He is quiet, thinking. He doesn't speak for a while. I hate it when he does that. It makes me nervous.

"Okay," he speaks, "we need to check your mental state to conclude everything, just to make sure you're not delusional." Great that's all I need, a shrink to inform me that my brain is going pop also. "It's more to do with the mystery behind your secret surgeon. Omar is the only one whom I know that can perform such an op in such a skilled manner. It's a bit old-school, but the technique is brilliant and full reconstruction and mobility should be restored. The goods news is that you can go home once we get the police off your back and get Dr O'Hara to check out your noggin." He taps his head and smiles. "Please, who did this?" His request is like a cross-examination. "We could do with a good surgeon. They are so difficult to get, and with Dr Omar away, it's difficult."

I think quickly and request to see the notes and info. He nods and replies that he will bring them by shortly. I accept his acknowledgement and, for once, his kindness for believing my story. I just have to wait for the loony party to arrive.

O'Hara was kind and confirmed that, of course, my brain was okay. However, they have to do a CAT scan just to make sure there is no malfunction. The police will have to wait until after the scan is completed. That is good news. I really have had a brain full of sheer nonsense so far.

At least my hand is healing quickly and easily.

The scan is scheduled ASAP and completed successfully without cause to be concerned. Mind you, the whole thing is really quite noisy and claustrophobic.

I am at last given the rite of discharge, with Simon, my forever best friend, to take me home. He was given leave from the ward rounds to do so. However, I'm confronted by the police at the exit of the hospital foyer. We are escorted to one of the more private rooms for discussion.

The sergeant introduces himself and begins. "It has been drawn to our attention that Mr John Finley would like to press charges against you, Miss Samantha Tomlinson of apartment 4 King George House, London. What do you have to say to the accusation that you had someone fix him up, so to speak, outside the Starbucks coffee plaza on Tuesday past. "

My jaw hits the deck and my blood is boiling. "What?!" I below. "What?! Have you seen what he did to my hand? I had to have an operation to get it fixed. He assaulted me." My face is now is brilliant red with rage.

"Calm down, miss. I am only requesting your assistance in this. He does have a broken jaw. And has been attended to at Whittington."

"Does it look like I could deck a guy with my build? Or even land a punch with my hand all stitched up already?" I was mad, really, really mad. The nerve of the guy. He put me out of work for a long time now, about a week or so. "Ask the young man that gave a statement at the time of his arrest. He said a passer-by came to my aid." Good thinking.

"Well, miss, it seems that Mr Finlay assumes this person knows you, as he called out your name as he punched him."

"What?! I didn't see the guy. And you know I am a nurse here; many people know me."

"I get your point, miss, but Mr Finlay is implicating it as a set-up."

"Bollocks," I swore at him. "This is complete bullshit. He is the one pissing about with other girls, and he dumped me on my birthday to go off with a Ryanair girl, my ex-flatmate, to Germany. Ask WPC Lindsey Gillingham. She saw the whole thing." Oops, too much venom coming out now. "I have been through hell and back with that guy. He attacks me out of the blue, and someone comes to my rescue, who I don't know, and then he gives me this shit." I stood up to leave. I glare at the officer, who now, in return, smiles at me.

"Thank you, miss. It appears that the gentleman we need to converse with is a doctor here. It also seems he knows you. Do you recall him, miss? He did bring you into the hospital. But when you're ready, miss. Come down to the station and place a full statement, and we can tie up the loose ends with the WPC. That will be all."

I stare at his eyes and wonder for a moment whether this is some sick joke of his to wind me up. The look I give gives my thoughts away.

"This is no joke, miss. We needed to see some reaction from you and hear your side so we can use the witness's statement of self defence and stop these bastards from abusing other peoples' rights." He smiled a reassurance at me as he stood up. In this instant, I wonder who could hear me swearing outside. "You should take care of that, miss. According to what the medical files say, that injury was quite nasty. And we took the picture evidence to help convict Mr Finlay further."

"Picture evidence?"

"Yes, apparently the surgeon was good enough to take x-rays and drawings of the injury and to give a full account of the details of what was done before in the glass injury and what Mr Finlay later inflicted. Pretty smart guy. Who is he? I'd like to be left in his hands, if I you know what I mean. Is he the chap the escorted you across the road?" He smiles again and gives me a good day.

I am stunned. I flop down into a chair and try to gain my composure. I start to tremble and then sob. There's a small knock at the door, and Simon enters with a large mug of sweet tea and a bundle of notes. For once, his arms are not flapping. "So, how did it go with Mr Truncheon?" He gives a little naughty laugh. "I sweetened him up with some of my extra special brew. Here, try some. He seemed quite nice. Why were you swearing at him?" His words are gentle but calmingly true. He pauses and then hands me a crumpled tissue from his pocket to wipe my eyes.

"It's a shame you're gay," I laugh. "You would make an excellent boyfriend." He now laughs really loud.

"I do make an excellent boyfriend. Sorry." He smiles. "I think of you more as my little sister." He reaches across and hugs me, passing the tea into my hand and removing the soggy tissue. "Well, guess what I found." He is all excited. "Well, given to me by Uncle."

He hands me the original notes that were found attached to the bed. I tremble as I put down the mug of tea and take the papers from Simon. I am stunned at the handwriting. I feel pale. My skin feels prickly and beads of sweat start to form on my forehead. "Jesus, you all right?" Simon panics. "You don't look good. Have some more tea." Then his arms start to begin again.

"No, I'm fine," I lie. But I can't help laughing in a hysterical way.

"It's impossible." I laugh again. "Impossible." I choke. Then a flash comes to me. "The hospital library – let's go now." I shoot up from the chair, hurling the papers at Simon, who has a stunned look of confusion on his face. "Bring those with you. I have something to show you." I grin but am worried about the CAT scan. Maybe they missed something.

Simon appears with a fresh set of contact lenses for me, which he acquired in the ophthalmic department. I pop them in. He says he will check with the coffee shop to see if my eyeglasses are there and if they are still in one piece.

# THE LIBRARY

We hurry along the corridors, and Simon asks what the hell am I doing and tells me I need to go home and rest. A big brother? More like a mother hen.

We reach the bay in the library, and the diary is still in my pigeonhole reserve. Either the assistant had been too lazy to put it back or she knew I would continue to read it. The other copy of the book is missing from my bag.

I plonk down on the desk in the far corner of the room. Simon is still questioning my sanity. "Give me the papers," I demand. He obeys. "Open the diary," I demand again. He opens it slowly and then his face plaids. We both stare down at the handwriting. It is one in the same.

"No, no, no." Simon's arms begin to twitch. "Impossible, creepy, weird, whatever you want to call it."

I read from where I set the bookmark in the diary.

> The image was of wonderment. She passed across the room in some shapely ghost formation, but her eyes seemed distant, troubled. I wondered at the image. She

paused and regarded me, as if seeing me as peering through a window. She raised a large glass of a generous helping of what struck me as white wine. I was stunned and responded back with my scotch glass. Then something oddly enchanting happened: she blew me kiss through the frame, and I read her lips through the silent glass, "Cheers! Drinks on me. Happy birthday!" She then disappeared like a figment of my mind. However enchanting the ghost was, she filled my room with the scent of roses, and an enlightenment overcame me; it could also have been the stress of working to put so many disfigured, tortured souls back together in body but never in mind. And now I am caught with the mindset of madness, but a little escapism never hurt anyone.

My hands are shaking. I am reading about myself. About me! In a book over sixty years old freaky!. Simon fell silent and is also reading the diary. "Go on, I want to see more," he encourages me. I regard him in silence. He hasn't taken his eyes off the page.

Today, a whole bundle of wretched victims were slammed on the porcelain. I was working till quite late. The infantry has demanded more men to fight against the Nazi regime, which means I must work my best to send some back to the front. I despise war, an issue that could be settled with intelligence and compromise. When you stand in blood-soaked gowns and work as on a factory repair line, you are supposed to block out the fact that these individuals will go back to war and come home just as mangled or worse. War – an atrocity to shame us as intelligent creatures.

It is late. I am at last free from my clothing and take a long, hot bath in front of the open fireplace to wash away the grime of the outside world. I stand to view my visage in the mirror to see what state my stubble has reached from the hours of work. I am wrapped in a towel and look into the other realm. I am shocked to see her. But this time, the room that reflects back is not mine. It is the same room, but the furniture is unusual and arranged such that it faces the wall towards the fire place.

There is something two people are observing. It has moving pictures similar to that of a small picture house. But the colours are bright and fast.

I can only see the back of her head. She is with company, but I assume they are not together as lovers, as the body language suggests a plutonic male and female, perhaps a brother and a sister.

## THE MIRROR

I burst out laughing and rib Simon. He shushes me to read on further.

> The girl, the beautiful girl, is weeping – a heartfelt weep it seems by the movements of her shoulders. A sadness, perhaps of a loss or hurt. They are consuming foods from cylindrical containers and guzzling wine. I stand there naked, pondering their plight. The man rises from his seat and approaches the mirror. He is, as I would say, a lady man: well kempt but definitely not a common man's friend. This explains the body language and the friendship involved. He is a comforter to her. She turns her head towards the back of the man and requests a refill, I think. He bounces his arms in an odd response in a positive manner. Her eyes are red and deep; there is something upsetting her. My heart lurches at the thought that something so beautiful could be so hurt. The young man stops to peer at his own face, but his eyes tell me he sees me. He is stunned at first but then blushes. His arms move in a beckoning manner to the girl. I am aware of my nakedness, and in response to the man's expression, I throw myself over to the sofa to hide my pride.
>
> I am again alone and acting like some mad fool. I laugh to myself and go back to my business of shaving off this damned

> cursed beard. But firstly, I will sit a while
> and smoke to relax in wonderment.

I lift my eyes from the diary and stare at Simon. He was telling me the truth. "This is weird," I comment, giving a slight, fractious laugh. "A ghost?" I ask him. "How can it be a ghost? That was last week."

Simon's lips are pressed tight. "Not a common man's friend," he spits.

"Oh, come on. Gay people were shunned into hiding, remember? You got shot if your gender orientation was really known. At least he is intelligent enough to realise that people have differences. See, he writes here about how much he hates war and has emotional feelings about the people he has to sew back together."

Now Simon turns on me. "You like him, don't you?" He waves his finger at me. "Bitch is straight and, my god, how well-hung."

I give him a disapproving glare. "Please, why does always have to be about sex or how big everything is? It's what you do with it that matters!" I state. I cannot believe we are arguing over male matters while reading about ourselves in some twilight zone. A shush is fired at us from the front desk. We giggle and then continue.

> I attempt to see Clive, my good friend,
> who is a thinking man. Alas, he has been
> called to the front to escort and analyse
> some of the poor victims blown down by
> the sick war. I really wanted his opinion on
> my mental state, whether I am working too

# THE MIRROR

hard or have a syndrome going off in the brain. I am imagining images in my mirror of a beautiful woman.

It is the following days after my birthday, and in early March, the rain is good for the soul. I am deployed from duty this day and am taking a long walk across to the park. It is some distance and a maybe a bit of stupid because of the chance of tripping on some unexploded weapon, but the day is pleasant and the rain good. I think of Clive being up to his ears in mud and grease and being undoubtedly deafened by the gunfire. I am a lucky soul to be based off-field and not on the frontline of madness.

I did request to assist nearer the action, but my skills as a surgeon are too damn precious to be torn apart by a Tommy gun by a Nazi bastard. The rain keeps my thoughts positive, and I am lost in a dream of the enchanting beauty in the mirror and its madness.

I return home to comb my hair. I gaze into the mirror and see my own reflection. I laugh and am disappointed in being alone. To hell with all the atrocities of war; to hell with it all. I slam on the gramophone, pour a glass of cognac, and puff heavily on some Samson tobacco. The best thing I find relaxing about my home is the nonsense of it all. Most of the apartments in this building are empty, with their occupants having fled to the countryside. So I can make as much rattle and din as I like without bother. I turn up the music and kick off my shoes. It's good old wartime songs again, but I love the Glen Miller music. It's a real upbeat tempo. "In the Mood"? Yep, in the mood for a party of fun with myself. I pace back and forth across the room, recounting ballroom steps and feel the urge to lighten the bladder. I am blessed with the luxury of indoors running water and a neat porcelain basin to sit upon comfortably. I stride dancing into the bathing room and am agog from what I find. The beauty, herself, is there, asleep, immersed in deep, richly perfumed water in the tin bath. There is music of a different element, fast and noisy. I tremble with fear; I do not know this place, and she is vulnerable. I can't help but gaze at her awhile, her beautiful porcelain body covered in petals and bubbles. Suddenly her head slips in and is submersed. I am seized by instinct and pull her head up. She gasps for breath, and then between her feet I see there is a water outlet, like the one in my butler sink. I pull it, draining the water away. She gasps and chokes, spilling water from her mouth. She clutches the sides of the tub and scrambles for a towel. I grab one from a warmed metal frame behind

> me, that is fixed to the wall and thrust it in her hand. She dries her face and opens her eyes to see me. Then she is not there. I am alone, peering into my tin bath. A shudder embraces my soul, and my heart lunges. I cannot forget such beauty and the beautiful curved bosom. I assure myself that no one can see me. I relieve my bladder in an undignified manner, fighting arousal.

Simon now giggles. "You didn't tell me about that, "he smirks, "giving him a boner in the bath."

"Simon, why does it have to be so, so…" I am blushing and shift uncomfortably in my seat. "Perv," I whisper.

"No, Miss Sammy-whammy, you like that, don't you? You prick–tease." He giggles again.

"Okay, I admit it's nice to know I have the body of a goddess."

"Nymph? More like nymphomaniac by what I have heard about you when you get your tongue into someone's mouth." He pokes me with his finger.

"Do you mind? What things being told about me?"

"Erm, let me see. That French student, Christian!"

"That figures," I storm. "He's a right fabricator."

"Apparently you go like a steam train." He smirks again.

"What? Wait a minute." I laugh now. He has bated me and taken me full in his joke. "You bastard." I jab him back.

We continue to read, even though I feel very uncomfortable with the story.

> I strip off and pour some more of the good
> stuff into a large glass and inwardly smile
> at my beautiful nymph. I pass the mirror to
> see if she is there and am aghast to see not
> her, but a stoutly faced female with metal
> objects like shrapnel attached to her face.
> Like some weird sort of pigmy with spears
> through its nose.

At this point I howl with laughter. Poor Jenny described as a pygmy. I guess the facial piercings can be somewhat of a shock. And Jenny is not the slightest of creatures, with her drinking of lager and trying to be one of the lads all the time. I whisper to Simon, "Don't you dare tell Jenny any of this."

A voice booms from the back of the library. "Tell me what?" Jenny snarls. Simon slams the book shut and guiltily looks down. "What?" she demands. A shush comes across from the desk. Now the assistant is walking towards us.

"Please leave. And quietly," the assistant demands. Great, Jenny spoils our fun. Simon is clutching the book and tries to sneak it out. I grab the paper files, trying to obscure them. The assistant snatches at the book and removes it from his clutch and puts it back under the desk into a pigeon hole for me. "If you wish to continue your studies here, miss, you must obey the rules." – a stern word from Adolf Hitler's niece.

"Cheers, Jenny," I retort in a fashion that could make a small child cry.

She starts to argue with me. "You were whispering about me. I know. I don't have big ears for nothing!"

"That's because of all that bloody junk you hang from it,"

spits Simon in my defence "You looked in the mirror lately? You're not far off from a pygmy!" He curls his lip and then heckles, "Don't come here upsetting Sammy; she's been through a lot."

"What did you call me, queer bitch?"

"I said, you cow hide, don't upset Sammy; she's had an operation because of that ex of hers."

"You said I am a pygmy! Right?" she bellows into his face with her teeth showing.

"Pack it in, please. For god's sake." I plead with them. They both turn away from their conflict, mouths open. "Someone take me home."

Jenny's tone changes rapidly. She is aware that she is still in uniform and that we are all in public view now in the corridor outside the libray doors.

"My car's out back. It will be more comfy than the crush." Her words are spoken in true kindness, showing the caring professional she really is. "You can take my car." She nods to Simon because she is still on shift. "Bitch bag," she snipes at him. She wanders off to get the keys from her station. Simon hurries back to the nurses' station to return the files to Uncle and tells me to go nowhere without him.

We meet by Jenny's old beaten up Fiesta. It's a fab, fun car with add-ons. She smiles sarcastically at Simon and then turns her serious face on to me.

"Thursday night." She smiles.

"What about it?" I am puzzled.

"You'll see," she smirks. "Stop all this hocus-pocus in your flat."

"That's tomorrow." I am stunned that she's carrying out her threat.

"Don't let him bend my wheels!" She glares at Simon.

Simon pokes his tongue out in rebellion. She hands over the keys and kisses me on the cheek. "See you about 8:00 p.m. Don't worry, it's nothing nasty or creepy," she jokes and she ambles back to the hospital entrance.

Simon snakes his eyes and mummers how much he dislikes that cow hide. But he drives the car steadily home.

# THE CARD GAME

I awake a few hours later on my sofa. I feel refreshed. The aroma of the tobacco is powerful and, for a fleeting moment, I think there is a party in my home. I walk to the bath and plop one of those fizz balls in it. I soak so long that my skin goes all wrinkly. My hand is wrapped in a polythene bag to keep the wound dry. I dampen down my skin with aloe moisturiser and feel so much more positive. To try and cover the wafting tobacco smell, I spray my favourite perfume around the bathroom and walk in and out of the spray to get an even fragrance over my body.

I wrap myself up like Cleopatra with the towel wrapped round my head. I open my bathroom door precariously in case there was some sort of party going on. But no, just me in a bath sheet and the smell of a gentleman's club.

I pause in the doorway and wonder if I should peek in the mirror. I look down at my hand and need to thank him somehow for helping me. I also need to warn him of Jenny the pygmy and the medium coming tomorrow. Silly how could I there be a way to find of communicating.

I stand in front of the mirror and saw only myself.

Nothing. But the aroma was so strong. I sit myself in front of the TV and flick through the channels. I find some old show about world war Twoand get engrossed. The pain increases in my hand, so I pause the screen on an image of Mussolini and Hitler and wander to the kitchen for a glass of water, a diazepam, and a co-proxamol. I return to the TV and unpause it. I am still trussed up as some mummy in robes. From where I sit, I smell cognac in my glass and for a split second I swear I can see my missing bracelet on the table in front of me. I reach to touch it but spill my water doing so. I get up to mop it with the towel around my head. As I start mopping it, the towel becomes stained with what appears to be cognac. It definitely smells of it. I freak out and run across the room to the mirror and see him.

The room has several official-looking gents in military uniform seated around a small table, all puffing away on various forms of lung cancer-inducing herbs. They are playing a serious card game, which looks like I have disrupted it. My water had splashed across a general's leg, not just any general but – my god – Eisenhower! What the hell is he doing here? The men are frantically trying to work out what has just happened..

A trick, no doubt, of a cheating card thief! I am bemused and sorry to cause such a problem. There is also two other men. My god, Churchill, I think. What the hell is he doing here? And it's his cognac that has vanished. Oh shit. I just stare into the scene. Then they all laugh, except Charles Hamilton Smythe, who looks up from the manic table and catches me, all bedraggled in my bathrobe and staring at them with an open mouth and wide eyes. He gives a little amused smirk at the incident. He mouths something, but I

# THE MIRROR

don't understand. He is a most handsome man I have ever laid eyes on.

I can see quite clearly he's sober. He picks up Churchill's glass and approaches the mirror, where he has moved his drink bar to be in front of. He is close now. He looks down naturally to fill the glass. Then he looks up directly into my eyes. If he was actually standing directly in front of me, he would be only inches away from my face. We share a moment between us, one of those that you can only express if you've felt it. I quickly put my bandaged hand up and say thank you. He smiles, saying nothing. But the look in his eyes tells me thanks. I try to speak more, but he turns his back, Churchill is booming for his glass. The game proceeds. I am getting cold and leave them to play. I put on my fluffy Winnie the Pooh pyjamas and carry on watching the story of World War II. Then it strikes me. What If I can change something in the past, like in that TV show *Quantum Leap*? I laugh loudly. I check the time to see it's past midnight now. I cannot smell the tobacco as strongly now. I go to the mirror to tell my friend the medium is coming and of the frontal attack on Dunkirk Beach. But what am I doing? If I relay the information, he will have to tell someone and then he will look like the Nazi spy they claim he is. Shit, what do you do?

I pose in front of the mirror like the queen in *Snow White*. I touch its frame gently and stare into it daring not to blink.

He is alone, asleep in the chair. Shit, I need to wake him up. I tap the glass, but the sound just vibrates back to me. Then a get an idea. I calculate his seated position in the reverse of the mirror and run to the kitchen for a glass of water. I throw it at table, but it just splashes and soaks my carpet. Now what? How did it happen before? I'm not sure. The carpet is wet, and in the process of throwing the water, I knocked over a vase of water. It stinks. So now I need to clean two areas of water spillage with one hand in a plastic bag. It really does smell, and I am all out of Febreze furniture cleaner, so I get the old favourite bottle of perfume out and start to spray the room. Then I become aware of eyes on me. I look up from my squatted position on the floor and smile at the rather dazed man in the mirror. I get myself up slowly but with dignity and approach the mirror.

Placing my hand on the mirror gently, I thank him again. He smiles, just smiles, and then points at my pyjamas. I laugh; they're quite funny. Twirling them in the mirror to give a flirty pose of the comfortableness of them, I almost topple over. His hands are both pressed against the glass as if to put them through it to stop me from falling. I put my hands against the glass where his are and smile. Then I remember what I need to tell him; he lips reads, which I know that from his diary. How much do I tell him? Where do I start with someone half-cut in another dimension? I start rambling stupidly. Then he does something odd. He leaves the mirror, and I am looking at his back. Then he moves to the side, and I notice he is not alone, but the other officer is poking his head over the side of the sofa. He's sloshed, but showing concern of the movements of my friend. I stand back from the mirror and place the towel I was using to clean up the spilt vase water, over it.

It is some minutes before I peek through the towel. The officer is leaving. My friend is hesitant to stand in front of the mirror; he seems twitchy about responding to me. Eventually he regains confidence and turns back to the mirror with a badly written note in his hand. It read: "I am being watched. All paranoid. xx".

I am shocked. They really did think he was some sort of spy. But almost all were in the war. I tell him that Jenny is coming with the medium and when the date is.

He looks oddly at me, his head cocked to one side in understanding. Then he asks to see my hand by pointing at it. Gently, I unwind the castings and lift it to the frame. He signals to rotate it, then okays me again. I mouth about his diary and about the hospital. He waves at me about something; he is distracted by a noise in the air. Then the image is lost. I cannot see him; I am alone again. Bed, sleep, pain relief.

# HIS OTHER ROOM

I am awake early and set off down to the library. I enquire about the book and begin to read again, only this time I feel I am prying.

> The incident with the pygmy woman has left me thinking of all the places I have not visited and should go once this damned war has finished.
>
> I sip my cognac and doze for a while across my ever-faithful sofa. I am woken by the sounds of a terrible screeching and the urgent smell of burning. I dash across to my bedroom to see if the boats below have been hit and to look through the blackout blinds to see if any air wardens are trying to rouse us dopey creatures. Nothing. I mean nothing. No boats below and the street is full of odd-looking folks all trussed up with short skirts, and its raining heavily.
>
> I rush back across the living room. I

# THE MIRROR

find myself somewhere different than my own apartment. Still the smell of burning is throttling my throat. It is the kitchen. There is smoke and flames tearing from beneath the grilling pan with the charred remnants of something once consumable. I open the window, rinse a tea towel with cold water and dampen down the very crispy object under the grill. I turn the gas off and my eyes begin to focus on the body lying in the floor. It's her. I pick up her small frame and rush back to the sofa. I check her vital signs. Her breathing has stopped, and I immediately resuscitate her. I feel somewhat foolhardy handling her, but saving is all I can do. I take note of the bleeding hand. It is severely wounded and much blood has been lost through the opening. I can hear people calling her name. I race back across the living room towards the entrance door... my door... her door and grab my suture case and medical supplies. Dashing back again in a furious panic, I almost trip on something, a shoe I think. I drop the kit but still have the case. I pull up her soaked sleeve and begin to remove the glass, squeezing her hand to stop the artery from spilling any more. I remove her bracelet and wrap it around my left wrist. I begin to work on mending the sliced ligaments and successfully stop the blood and seal up the wound. I can still hear the annoying sound from the kitchen and the people at the door screaming her name. Her name: Samantha. I now know her name.

I am squatted down next to her when eventually the door bursts open and the lady boy is there, flapping his arms. He rushes to the kitchen, then dashes my way. He freezes, staring at me aghast, and then he looks at Samantha in horror. I am then suddenly alone, kneeling next to my own chesterfield with her bracelet around my wrist. Samantha's bracelet. What a weird moment. I check to make sure that I am not dreaming. My hands smell of iodine, smoke, and her perfume. In fact, I can still smell her in the space. But where is this? I cannot recall the past history of this place. The building is fairly new, well the '20s. I am perplexed. Her room was plush with soft flooring, warm for this time of year too, and what the hell was that strange contraption she sat in front of that produced pictures? What was happening? How? Why? I am in a dangerous position to be doing strange things or acting odd. But she... her skin smelt of flowers, and although her breath was of intoxicated and smoke-filled, her lips were so soft I wish that it was a kiss of passion rather than of giving life.

Now it is I who am the intruder. The guy saved my life twice and gabbles on as if I am some supreme woman. I am blushing at the thoughts this man had without even knowing or understanding me. Drawing a deep breath, I look up around me to see if there are any spies, as I am getting wartime paranoia, but even so it is embarrassing reading about oneself in such a manner. Why would he write down such thoughts? People who are alone or afraid do that sort of thing. I laugh quietly and realise I am questioning my own habit. The diary continues:

> Perhaps the fun of the cognac has encased me, or maybe I should stop smoking so much or stop the occasional opium pipe, as I am sure it does me no good.
>
> It has been several days since seeing her. I hope and pray that she is well. When I look into the glass, I see only myself. I ponder her existence: where she is and what she is doing now at this moment. Samantha of the looking glass. Churchill has elected a group of troops to go along the French frontier, which means, of course, we have to make the hospital shifts easy for the military personnel to be attended too. Smaller operations have been cancelled and my work is concentrated on the more urgent cases. I see each one as urgent, because if someone is injured, it is an urgency to them. We had three stillbirths

on the maternity wing today, and I was given the purposeful questions of why. Perhaps the water is affecting the foetus' growth. It could also be the malnutrition due to the local rationing of food sources. These women are thin and gaunt, without men to hold their hands at such a tragic time in their lives. Some who gave birth to their dead son or daughter would have lost two lives in that short incident of life. How tragic, how sad a species we are to try to eliminate each other over lands and dictatorships.

And yet, my mind ponders where she is, wondering if she is safe and well. What has happened to her voluptuous body?

I take a walk this morning in the rain to clear my head from all the sadness around me. I return to my apartment and find the remnants of her previous day's fire. I am puzzled. Something is adrift here. And I clean the kitchen – her kitchen – the broken glass I wrap up in paper and I scrub down the walls. It has strange wonderful components, all neatly packed into tiny spaces. There's a large metal object with cooling facilities. I open the door and it is full of wonderful ingredients: apples, grapes, ham, cheeses, bread, and butter in small containers. I take an apple and bite into it with vigour. It is sweet, so sweet my

## THE MIRROR

mouth drools and I need to wipe away the juice. I can't help but take a knife from one of the stream-lined drawers and plunge it into the wedge of cheese. The cheese is gooey and almost stings my mouth with its rich flavour. It has a label: Gorgonzola. I see wine sitting in the door of the cooling cupboard, and I cannot resist. Glasses, I see, are neatly secured behind a cupboard of glass and are resting on a glass shelf. I take one down and pour some of the wine. I glug it; it too has a light, sweet bouquet, refreshing my pallet. I observe the rest of the room's layout.

There is an electrical stove and large, shiny metal pots, one with a bowl-shaped window containing a cylindrical drum.

I may be a man, but I can do house work and tidy as I go. I stash an apple in my pocket, as well as a small chocolate bar.

I tidy her living area and cannot help but rummage through her books and hunt for clues as to who she is or what she is and where she's from. I pace around the bookcase and am amazed to see what I do: books, all jammed together, from history to photography, from romance to literature. Then I find it: her diary. It has a hard cover with brightly coloured swirls and the year on it My mind races. How could I be in such a time so far away from my own? I must be over a hundred now if I was alive in this era and if it was correct of my thinking of when I was. It all bemusing .. I open it with trembling hands and start my enquiry. She is a nurse at the same hospital as I, but I do not recall her name. I would have certainly remembered her. Her friend is what is known as gay. Gay, what a strange word to describe him. Happy? She has a bad relationship with some one called Johnnie. I guess he is the thug in the photo on the mantle piece. He sounds to me as if he requires a good beating.

As soon as I am engrossed, I can hear footsteps approaching. I quickly look up into the mirror. It hangs in her room exactly where it hangs in mine. A flash of cool goose pimples run over me, my stomach knots and I find myself back on my side of the mirror, watching her view the room's tidiness in bewilderment.

I pause to gather my thoughts lightly touching the mirrors frame. I am slightly annoyed at someone poking around in my business, but hey, that's what I am doing right now.

He continues to explain some of the poor issues and the starvation, the parents having to send their children outside London for a safer home. I remember my grandmother saying she was carted off to Cornwall and had a fantastic time, but on returning to London, it nearly broke her heart to see all the mess. She had lost her eldest brother in the front. It filled me with a great deal of questions about 'have we ever learned to really appreciate our nosey neighbours' or the fact that the politicians are not always right. Look at Chamberlain; he got strung along by Hitler. A shudder runs down me. I am certain I am being scrutinised. I continue looking at his writings. Again, a description of a surgical procedure. I think this is totally amazing. The diary is spooking me into a false sense of something I have not felt. Weird but wonderful.

# CHARLES AT THE COFFEE SHOP

Today I took a walk along the path from the Herb Garrett and found myself enraptured in a small Underground square I had never seen before. I am stood, even poised perhaps in the entrance arch. I scan across the vast vibrant station, and am bemused in wonderment . The structure itself , new polished simulated marbled walls, with metal gating poles at the entrance into the stations esculators, people are bustling through with some sort of recognition card, they tap onto a pad at the top of the pole. An automated system, clunking and beeping. Metal gates opening and shutting , grunting as they slamb closed. It is something of a dream of science fiction. The floor gleaming clean highly polished slabs a true wonderment itself. Outside it was raining a light drizzle, but the place was teaming with people of

# THE MIRROR

all sorts of races and colours going to and fro, all busy. Busy folks, bustling. They all were dressed in an unusual, unfamilar manner. Some were dressed very odd indeed. The women had clinging revealing tops , trousers, and skirts that left nothing to the imagination. It blew my mind, even the gents were wearing a mix of shirts and ties and trousers that hung so low that their underpants wereon display. Indeed what sort of attire was that? The people were busy, moving in a fast pace pushing and shoving with very little manners. Women who were dressed in brightly coloured saris(I beileve that what they are called were pushing odd pramalaters that had three wheels. The children undisciplined squeeling in high pitches of chaotic disorder. They spoke in languages unfamiliar to me. There were huge, dark black men with the most amazing hair, all twisted, matted, and flowing like it was alive. Some people were holding small contraptions that they were talking into, shouting and babbling like mad men one man was swearing and ranting quite disturbingly. There were conversations of madness, laughing, shouting, andof negotiation.

Some people appeared alien-like. They were so big they were struggling to walk, awkwardly waddling, heaving their bodies in painful steps. One person whizzed past me on a motorised chair, nearly knocking me over. It was all a very strange. For a horrific fleeting moment I thought I had found a crazy Nazi camp or had stumbled upon a looney bin. I caught the eye of a newspaper seller,by tipping my hat. He is staring at me, his mouth gaping. I, in my attire of hat, case, umbrella, and cloak I must have looked a strange sight to him indeed amidst the other folks . Although he appears odd to me with his dark meditterian skin and hair, greek looking at a guess.

Then I smelt something most wonderful. Coffee and the gentle aroma of pastries. It wasn't just coffee, but it was pure, aromatic, unadulterated coffee. I am immediately drawn to it.My attetion is then drawn back . The headline of the paper astounded me: 2012 OLYMPIC SCAM. OBAMA TO QUIT HIS TEAM.

Who is this and what does it mean? I try to read the front of the paper, but the seller rebukes me, requesting that I pay. He then questions, in an ungentle manner, where the hell I came from. Was I part of some magician's team? I cannot recall the name he suggested. I tip my hat in apology again and bid him good day. I do notice that no one is smoking inside, instead they are bedraggled and away form the entrance, furiously inhaling neatly trimmed cigarettes, from shiney angled boxes or packets. I have never heard of the names on the boxes, and as I pass, I see some form of a warning label printed on the packets' side. I reach for my trusty tin , from inside my cloak, to ignite my own self-rolled tobacco and once more am rebuked by the newspaper seller. He points to the sign at the entrance and quotes to me that what I am doing is against the law. How bizarre. What harm is there in a cigarette , the red indians have smoked tabacco for many hundreds of years, without complaint, in matter of fact as medicinal .

My mind and olfactory sense are then drawn back to the coffee aroma. I tip my hat again in a polite gesture and take leave of the gent, igniting the tabacco outside as requested. The aroma, it's coming from close proximitly. The last time I smelt something so wonderful was in Paris many years ago. I wander out towards the aromatic scent like the pied piper is leading me.

There she is,

alone, sipping coffee from what appears to be a cup made from paper.

My heart skips.

My skin pricks with delight.

Her hand movement is good; it is dressed in clean bandages, a light-weight sort. I am thrilled to see her. I try to cross the corner of the street, but the traffic is strange — fast ,busy, noisy. A young man nearly runs me down on his sleek, stream-lined, most amazingly powerful motorcycle. I tip my hat in apology. He just waves and murmurs something from behind his tortoiseshell-shaped helmet. Then, as I approach, the man I saw in the photograph,(the thug) is confronting Samantha. He grabs her poor hand crushing it. She wails in pain, letting a high pitched squeal , begging him to let go. "Leave her alone!" I boom. My pace quickens, a young man behind her yells at him to leave her alone.

I guess this is Johnnie. He has a vicious snarl across his face. He is enjoying administering the pain. I call out her name and strike the snarling creature across his jaw in such a fashion that causes much discomfort, pain, and deformation to that horrid look in his eyes. He is out cold. He clatters amongst the cast-iron tables, spilling his blood. She is gasping.

I am alone again in the rain, amidst the rubble of a building that has been blown to bits by bombs.

My head is confused. I yearn to find her. I run down the streets, knowing how stupid I appear as I call her name. I cross the corner. The rain is hard now, and my coat is drenched. There, she is staggering, doubled in pain. Her face pallid, contorted. A policewoman is helping her.

The rubble remnants of blitzed buildings have disappeared. Once again, it's all new and strange. But I understand where we are. I cross over to assist.

I grab her, stopping her from fainting into the road. I pull her to her feet. There is some misunderstanding. I am a doctor, I explain to the policewoman, She does not seem to believe me. An agreement is made. I do not quite understand. I have to give a statement at the station after I look after the victim. The policewoman then informs me the bastard needed a good pasting, and she winks at me. Johnnie is being put in the back of a police van. His face bloodied, delirious, dazed, but his words are harsh, disgraceful, shocking.

The policewoman allows me to wrap Samantha up in my coat and escort her back across the road to the hospital. I smile and thank the policewoman politely. She obliges and informs me to take good care of Samantha; she calls her "a good one." The policewoman returns to the coffee shop and continues with her enquiries.

We reach the hospital. It looks all familiar again. I call a staff nurse and prepare Samantha for surgery. By her movement and the pain she experiencing, I can see the

> hand is damaged severely. I hate that man. He should be on the front, being stitched up by some mad Nazi doctor.
>
> We rush down to the theatre; I take extensive notes of her condition before and after the incident, x-ray her, and then get the staff to find the hospital artist. She is stable, frightened, and pallid. I haven't had a chance to fully speak with her. Each time we meet, she is in trouble. What did God have intended. I leave the notes on the foot of her bed. I sense she will disappear again. Alas, she is tormented each night by the bombardment; she wails hysterically, crying in pain and in an odd language of gibberish. I have no choice but to sedate her, to keep her calm and safe whist her hand heals. She is a good patient when she's awake; she eats, drinks, and conforms to using the bedpan. However, as the sedative leaves her body, she panics, causing chaos in the ward. Sister Eunice keeps a careful watch over her.

"Excuse me, miss," a voice calls to me. "We close in five minutes. The students have a lecture here this afternoon." It is not the usual old bag. Her face is kind and warm, a bit like my gran's was. "You've been here all day. What's intriguing about..." She cranes her neck round to see what I am reading. "Oh, didn't know we had Doc Smythe's diary. He went off to the military for while for decoding. All that weird stuff he wrote about..." She sighs and continues. "Mind you, he put it right for us young'uns to get fresh clean water and extra rations for me ma when she was having our David."

"How old are you?" I enquire gently. "Sorry, rude question."

She smiles gently. "That's alright, love. A lot older than you think. I do this because I get bored at home watching TV. And that old bag in here goes off sick every now and again." She laughs. "Perhaps she could go permanently, by what I hear about her."

I cheekily ask her, "Can I borrow this?" She shakes her head.

"Sorry, love, not that one. There is a copy."

"Yes, I have it, but it's not the same in print as reading it in his own handwriting."

"Know what you mean, but the book's too precious to the history of this place."

I glance over the diary, intrigued as to what our next adventure will be. I wonder around the hospital and head for the coffee bar.

# THE SÉANCE

It is at the other coffee bar near to the hospital that I see her,. Ryanair big boobs. She looks up and smirks and then continues to chat with her friend. I feel rage in me. Then it changes to sympathy; she is dating a monster. Or is she one too? I then laugh and think of them as two ogres.

I am no longer intimidated by either her or Johnnie. I pass her by, order my coffee, and ignore her completely. I can hear hard-spitting words coming from her mouth, and then she retorts about how wonderful it was to be shagging Johnnie in my bed when I was off on shift. I want to turn and lump her one, but I am in no fit state to be getting into a punch-up. A young business woman addresses the bitch and pipes in that she didn't leave her office to listen to some old slut's story when her head is filled with far more important details of the business nature. I am now smirking into my cappuccino. I blow the froth off as I pass the three of them and wink at Ryanair.

Wow, that felt good.

I stop off for some sushi on my own. The sushi bar is not

quite buzzed up yet, and the chef has his undying attention on me.

I ask where everyone is. He says most folks come down a little later on Thursdays. He says he remembers me from before. I enquire from where. He flashes a wink as if I would remember. Then it clicks. He cut off one of his fingers late one Saturday night whilst I was on A&E shift. We laugh. He then says something very strange: "Many a things come to the heart from another soul."

"Beg pardon?" I don't understand. He laughs.

"You will soon see," he winks. "You have a good spirit. I see it. Yes. A good spirit. You will find him again." With that he carries on chopping. I stare at him.

He looks up to regard my puzzlement at his words. "Thank you for fixing me." He grins.

I am bewildered. I say "no problem" and leave him a good tip.

As I pace up the stairs, he bellows, "Wait and see. Won't be long. You'll see."

The séance. Shit. What am I going to do with Jenny? I look back at the chef who is waving his cleaver at me, smiling. I go to ask what I am going to do. He smiles and says, "Go with peace. It will work itself out!" He laughs again. "Wish I could be there."

Freaky. I shake my head and trudge upwards out the bar with a belly full of raw fish and a séance to attend. My life changed the day I hung that mirror. What was with it, anyway?

I am greeted on my homestead front by Jenny and a strangely dressed woman. She looks like Rose from Blackpool Pier, the type that tells you what you want to hear. I smile politely at Jenny's scowl and whisper, "Humour me," and give a strained laugh. The woman speaks soft and slow, in lower whisper than me.

"Tonight, truths will be told." I glance into her deep, sunken eyes.

"Come on up," I encourage them. What am I doing? I just hope in my heart that something is bigger than this strange evening.

I open my door with bated breath. What will I find? And what will the stranger behind me wearing 1970s living room curtains find? Yes, I think they hung in my old neighbour's house across the cul-de-sac. If I remember correctly, she had the biggest fat cat I had ever seen. But, mind you, I was only five at the time. That house was in a time warp, and sadly she died a few years ago. My aunty said the curtains were burned by the relatives. My heart sinks. A lonely old woman with her fat cat.

"My name is Francesca Rossini, my dear." My thoughts are dragged back to the little fat woman. Her face is jowly, reddish from the constant Christmas sherry, I guess. Our eyes meet. She gasps. "So much light and energy. Your aura is amazingly brilliant." She leans towards me. "It draws them to you," she whispers in that freakish low voice like from some Spielberg movie.

I roll my eyes and reply, "Tea, biscuits, or a glug of chardonnay?" I politely point them to the table, which still has last night's wine glass, half empty, poised on the edge.

The kitchen is immaculate again, cleaned with precision, and a small card has been left in the corner. It has what I can only describe as a little face drawn on it, a smiley. My heart lurches; I am unsure myself of what the hell is going

## THE MIRROR

on. The one thing I know is I like my haunting, and this little, fat busybody isn't going to spoil my fun. I put the kettle on, assuming the medium doesn't drink because it dulls the senses. My thoughts are disturbed again by the imposers. I am aghast to see the pair of them viewing the mirror as I poke my head out from the kitchen.

"Tonight's fashion night!" I boom in perfected sarcastic sentiment. Jenny gives the finger and sharply sits\ back at the table. The short, fat, round woman stands there stroking the mirrors edges like it is some pet. "Kettle's on!" I project my voice at the medium. "Tea, coffee, whisky?" I can't help the flow of gears at them both. Hostile is a good word to describe how I feel.

Rossini peers back at me and replies, "Whatever is least inconvenient for you." Her words cutting.

I shrug my shoulders and return to my duties. Jenny is quick behind me. I brace for the tirade of how rude I am. A rap at my front door startles us. I huff past Jenny to answer.

A youngish girl stands there with a bewildered look. I say she was probably seventeen years old but has a real baby face. The girl shifts from one foot to the other. I stare at her, willing her to speak.

She stammers, "Er, well, this sounds, well, er, are you Samantha Tomlinson?"

I nod with curiosity. The girl's face flushes; she then bellows over the banisters, "Hey, Mark, you owe me a tenner! Bring it up!"

"Bring what up?" I retort. "And what bet?" My voice is slowly becoming surly. In a few moments, the young man arrives behind the girl, his arms billowing with enormous lilies.

It is the biggest bouquet I have ever been presented with. The girl, smiling, hands me a card. It is old and yellowed. She waits for me to open it. The whole charade is odd, the way the two people are acting. I oblige and open the card:

To Samantha,
I hope your evening goes well, love Charles. xx

My face reddens. I thank the girl. She then asks what it said. I rebuke her nosiness. She begins to explain, "My great-gran used to own the flower shop, and she made each one of us swear to deliver these flowers. She said a gentleman of odd curiosity paid a lot of money for the delivery in the future and, erm, well, it has been a family joke till now. Who are you, miss?"

I give a sharp, unbelievable laugh. "Simply Samantha Tomlinson."

She cocks her head to one side, noting Jenny behind me. "You're not like in one of those movies, are you?" she suggests, peering at Jenny's stunned visage.

"Like what?" I retort. Then I politely ask her to leave. The attention is drawing both guests to the door. I except the flowers from the young man and firmly close the door to find Rossini curiously viewing the flowers. The card is hidden in my leather jacket pocket.

I flaunt them at her. "Someone loves me." Rossini's eyes narrow with suspicion.

I retreat back to the kitchen. "Well, who are they from?" Jenny's voice also has suspicion in it.

"Nobody you know or understand," I retorted with venom. Our fracas is interrupted by Rossini's firm voice.

"Forget the tea. Can we get down to business, children?"

Jenny's face is a picture. "Children..." she utters, turning on her heels to sort out the insult. I lay the bouquet down on the kitchen table, smiling deep within my heart. How fantastic, mad, strange. I laugh. What a guy! I lay the card next to the bouquet.

Before I can take out the vase, there is another rap at the door. I roll my eyes and venture to the door, smiling politely at my guests.

This time it is a spotty-faced pizza delivery boy. "Pizza for Tomlinson. Deep-pan Hawaiian special, extra garlic bread, bottle of Diet Coke, and chocolate chip Häagen-Dazs."

"I didn't order," I reply.

His face is stunned, but it's probably not the first time it has happened to him.

"It's okay, miss. It was paid for. I was asked to deliver it, that's all." He shoves the box at me.

Then the penny drops. Simon. The chocolate chip Häagen-Dazs does it. His favourite. I smile embarrassingly at the boy, tip him, and close the door.

Jenny is fuming. "You're doing this on purpose. Whether Madam Medusa here called us children or not, it is rude and not funny, Sam. Its cost me good money to get the witch here, and you're just flaunting around, insulting us."

"I didn't ask or invite the so-called witch to come and do London's most haunted." I boom back at her, thrusting the pizza into her hands. "Perhaps you had better help me with eating this since you are so tetchy." Oh, I know how to hit Jenny's nerve. She puffs up her checks at me.

"Will you please come sit!" Rossini is loosing patience. "I sense something!"

Jenny obeys, taking the food with her. I stand for a moment and sense it too.

Suddenly, a massive boom is heard. The whole building shakes, the lights flicker, and then we smell the terrible aroma of burning. I stare at the two women. Rossini's face is pallid and Jenny is gawking at me.

My throat is choking with the smoke, but the two women are breathing regularly. Rossini gives instructions to Jenny by gesturing. I have trouble hearing their words. All I can hear is loud booming, the crackling of flames, and a wail in the distance of something horrid and frightening. The boom, it's deafening. I cup my hands, shielding my ears. I am terrified. Then I need air to breathe. I run across to the balcony with Jenny trying to rugby tackle me as I pass her.

Samantha rushed across the room, passing between the fingers of the two women like a ghostly shape. They reached out to touch her, but the attempt was futile. Samantha was like air; her clothes, her bag, all were a projected image.

She reached the mirror, gazed into it, and simply vanished into thin air.

The two women, panicked by what they had witnessed, searched the room in vain. The medium turned her attention to the mirror and stared into it, trying to fixate some source of energy. She was not amused that the object didn't surrender up anything to her powers of persuasion.

# THE RAID

Samantha is horrified. She is alone in the flat. It is filling with smoke and floating ash debris. The noise outside is thundering, deafening, terrifying. She freezes by the edge of the balcony; broken glass is splintered under her Doc Marten boots, some is twisted in her hair. It is pitch-black. Her heart is racing, her stomach is knotted tight. The noise is so deafening, that wailing noise; the booms are relentless, thumping her core.

She lets out a high-pitched, blood-curdling scream, cupping her ears.

Her eyes scan for light, anything. There are no flames or fire.

Her throat is scorched by the fumes; she's choking on brick dust and tarp smoke. Her mind is racing, slowing down her thought patterns.

The crackling of licking flames is devouring the wood grain.

Her scream stops as suddenly it began.

Taking in a huge lungfuls of the ashen air, her lungs rebel with a hacking cough. She's clasping her hands over her mouth now. Panic has no time to rear its ugliness. Her mind is fighting every want to scream again.

Her feet are frozen; her legs set as lead. Sudden pain in her hand snaps her back to reality. "Come on, Sam... think," she whispers to herself.

The bag is still on her shoulder. "Yes," she elates, and she expels a smaller, controlled cough. There is a small torch attached to her flat keys, a habit that she started after being in a blackout on the Underground. She fumbles for the bag, pawing at its contents. There it is. She grabs it with her left hand from way down inside the inside pocket. The bag is tipped up at a curious angle. Something falls from it, thudding on the slatted floor. No carpet. A curious thought. With the keys dangling from the end of the tiny torch, she presses it on and swirls the bright LED beam around the room.

Her mouth drops open in shock. "My God, where the hell am I?"

There, in the corner opposite the balcony window, the beam hovers on a slumped, dark figure. The shape moans. It is disorientated and in pain. Aghast at the scene, her heart pauses then suddenly quickens. She sprints to the figure. He's barely conscious, responding slowly to her shaky voice. She commands him to his feet.

The room is filling with throttling smoke and dust.

Finding a foot hold, Samantha dabs the moisture on his forehead with the edge of his sleeve. The wailing and droning outside increases; the solid booming quickens. She hears the grinding drone of something sinisterly mechanical, something relentless and tormenting that panics both of them. They quicken to find an exit. Urging the man to move faster, she supports him under one arm and races for the door. The man gestures to a leather Gladstone bag in the doorway. The bag is weighty and cumbersome. It unbalances her and slams both of them into the doorframe. They regain their senses, and the man grabs the bag from her with his free arm. Still swirling the torch, she sees the door is heavily bolted. The man props the Gladstone against the wood panel. Coughing at the billowing smoke, he yanks hard to release the catches. The latch lifts and the door groans inwards. A cloud of smoke swirls around them. They grip each other. She puts the torch into her mouth and heaves through the door.

The top of the staircase is full of sooty smoke, dust, and an acrid stench. Still with the torch in her mouth, she begins the intrepid journey downwards into the main foyer. The banisters are split like match wood and the stairwell creaks reluctantly, as if under a great strain.

Their footsteps are steady but quickening. They reach the fore doors. The doors are recast metal with small panes for windows, but the glass is broken out. She yanks hard against the door's floor bolt, and it releases them to the freedom of a burning South Bank.

Samantha freezes momentarily at the licking flames of the bombed-out building next to the flats. She wonders what the building had contained – lots of wood, perhaps – but the acrid smell suggests something more sinister.

Charles Smythe coughs, regaining his senses. He stands upright. "Put out the light." His words are in a gentle whisper but firm. Samantha releases his bag and her hold on him, removes the torch from her mouth, and flicks it off. They then gaze at each other and give a weird, stifled laugh.

For a second, Samantha gazes up at the flat window. She swears she can see Jenny and the medium. Jenny gazes at her friend, horrified, pallid, and screaming words unheard. She is concerned and calling her friend back. Rossini stares blankly skyward, petrified. Horror strikes Samantha's heart. What if her friend is trapped? However, the images are ghostly for a second and then fade. Sam gazes up into the sky and her heart freezes in utter horror. As far as her eyes could see, the sky was filled with aircraft. They were smaller planes than were normally flying in and out of London City Airport. Then she understands what the horrible sound is: the terrible mechanical grinding of the propellers.

A hand gently squeezes her elbow, and her thoughts are returned to the ground. Their eyes meet. He smiles very softly. "Will you be fine?" he enquires. His accent is unfamiliar, haughty and Eton. "We must leave here," he urges. "There is a shelter partway from London Bridge to Southwark. We need to go; it's a bad one tonight." He looked skyward. "They're incendiaries, mainly, but the last one was full loaded for the factory. Lucky it missed the house." His eyes gaze back towards Samantha. She noted the blood trickling down his brow.

"You're hurt. You're bleeding!" She points at his open scalp. He dabbed it again with his shirt sleeve.

"There's been worse." He shrugged. "Best we go. The concentration seems to be on the river and docks. We are not safe here." He leans down and grabs his bag. The air rings with relentless noise; the wind is filled with an acrid burning stench. The blackness is attacked by the flashes of explosions. Samantha heads left from the house, but Charles yanks her back towards the right. His face is bewildered by her action. "There's a shortcut through the side alley," she explains, bellowing over the thunderous booming.

He shakes his head. "There is another factory site there for the Waterloo Bridge. "

"Oh," Sam surrenders. "Of course... it got blown up by the doodlebugs... which is later." As her words slip out, Charles stares into her eyes, disbelieving his ears.

She smiles uncomfortably and replies to his glare, " I read a lot. I love history and —" Her words are cut short by a yelling, reprimanding voice.

Charles draws her close to him and whispers, "Be careful what you say. It is 1942."

The silhouette of a burly, heavy-set man with a jauntily placed tin helmet appears from the corner of the road. His words are still booming over the din, and his arms are waving, beckoning them to him. They obey his command despite not being able to clearly hear his inaudible instructions. A whizzing sound closes in, and Charles's pace quickens, frightening Samantha with its urgency. The ground shudders under the strain of an exploding force, blinding both companions temporarily. The silhouette is still bellowing at them. The explosion comes from behind the huge house and is followed by smaller popping bursts of gas.

Breathless, they reach the ARP, who is not amused at the two companions. He glances at the gapping wound on Charles's head. He then scowls at Samantha. He booms at them, "Come on, it's a bloody mess out here. Let's get you under shelter." He scowls again at Samantha "Where're your gas masks? And, miss, did you not have time to get dressed? May cause a stir like that." He then scowls and winks at the same time to Charles.

Samantha ponders the comment for a moment. Then it dawns on her. Her close-hung jeans must look like thick tights in the silhouette of night. She gives a slightly embarrassed laugh and then takes hold of Charles's arm.

The ARP marches them briskly down London Bridge towards the air raid shelter. Samantha, trying to keep her cool, cranes her neck relentlessly skyward. The air is filled with the malicious Messerschmitt Bf 110, which looked like swarming bees as they attacked helpless victims below. The sky is strung with barrage balloons, and massive antiaircraft guns rumbled from the tops of taller buildings, hurling endless debris skyward. Her mouth is dry and her belly is full of salty fish. Her mind is spinning. She clutches her stomach in its tight pain and it releases its contents.

They pause momentarily for her to regain control. She felt stupid, helpless. Warm words spill from Charles's lips to comfort her but also to urge her to quicken. "Keep going, we can do this. Thousands have, and we can too. Keep focused ahead. Don't look skyward." He squeezes his arm around her waist.

"You're still bleeding," she faintly whispers.

"You're that old doctor, Smythe," the ARP interjected for distraction. "Saved my sister's life two weeks ago. She lost a leg in a bombing, over on the estate at Elephant and Castle. Nearly bleed to death." His accent was strong East End, but he was sincere.

Cocking his head to one side, he smirked. "So, er, you and the good old doc here are associates?" For a brief moment, Sam blushed, realising the true meaning of his remark. With her brain addled by what had just happened to her, she didn't truly understand the entirety of the situation.

She responded with dignity. "I am a nurse at the same hospital. He wanted me to come around to ensure my hand was healing. Because the shifts change so quickly, it's so hard to get to see the same surgeon." She waved her hand at him quickly.

The man replied, "Good job you called in. He would probably be dead. Do not need such a surgeon to go amiss." He smiled sweetly as he stepped off ahead of them. "Funny uniforms they give you nurses these days. Thought she'd come out undressed. Beg your pardon, sir." He chortled with a cough and a tip of his helmet.

There was no more time to conduct any pleasantries as the sky above continued to drone.

Sam realised that what she was wearing what must seem bizarre attire to the ARP and felt somewhat self-conscious. Peering down at her bright red chunky boots, skin-tight denim jeans, a low-cut wrap top with sequins embroidered on it, the black leather embossed jacket, and, of course, the huge leather bag slung over her shoulder. Let alone the huge dangling earrings.

The ARP trudged off into the smoky air, still bellowing commands of urgency. The deafening noise droned on. She turned her attention towards the debris-spattered road. The sky continued its terrifying horror. Her legs, now light and flighty, sped up her pace, and Charles's body expelled a gentle sigh of relief. The sky was alight with an eerie orange glow with swirling clouds of thick black smoke and dust from the bombed-out buildings. Sam held her breathe, holding back a scream.

The air raid warden sharply led the way to the entrance of the concrete church hall. It was reinforced with concrete and many types of material to support and protect the occupants within. A home guard officer was at the doorway, awaiting the ARP to usher in the two trembling souls for the night.

They were greeted with a command. "Where're your papers?" the sergeant demanded. "Crap, "thought Sam, "this is going to be interesting."

Behind the sergeant, a black tarpaulin hung blocking any light from escaping. "Come on, come on," he demanded.

"Can we first come in and clean up this man's wounds, please? He is bleeding heavily," her voice and words were sharp and pointed.

Charles was aghast at the tirade of fiery words from something so slender and stammered, "Please, good sir, I can barely stand much longer."

The sergeant then called behind him, "Injury, we need a medical officer right away." His words were then gentle. "Come on, girl, get him inside." He lifted the heavy black cloth and summoned the medical officer again.

Inside, it smelt of body odour, dampness, and defecation from overused toilets. The air was thick and sticky; it smelt of stale tobacco stubs. The tenants were unconcerned to be inhaling the blue smoky air of the residence's chimney. Some were blowing smoke rings to amuse themselves. Others were nervously dragging cigarettes to a short stub in several long draws. Samantha choked and caught herself from almost gagging on the air. She waved her hand in front of her face, which was of no avail for clearing the stale, stagnant air.

They carefully stepped down into the shelter, leaving

some of the booming noise behind them. They entered into the dimly lit and cramped hall. A voice demanded, "You got a ticket?"

"What now?" thought Sam. Another officer of the home guard was assisting an ARP within the hall. The medic arrived and attained authority over the situation. The medic was a younger lad than the older gentry, and he smiled softly at Samantha. He guided them to a spot near the wall and shooed the couple that were already nestled there to move somewhere else. Charles slumped down hard, banging his back against the damp concrete wall..

"What happened? It's a nasty gash," the medic spoke softly, his accent well-bred, of Dorset, England.

Sam shook her head sadly. Her ears were still ringing from the deafening boom and crackle overhead. The stench of damp, overcrowded, sweaty bodies raised an acrid taste in the back of her throat, and she exhaled a gasp for fresh, clean air.

Sam thanked the medic for his concern and explained, "I am a nurse. I can attend his wound if you need to help others." She pawed at Charles's gaping wound.

The medic said, "I 'm a student at the Royal Infirmary. They are hoping to get me to the front, or better yet, British Polynesia, India, or even out to our posts in Burma over the next year. That is if I pass my exams and complete my training. It will probably next summer, if we are still at war. What do you think?"

Charles rolled his eyes in pain from the wound and the inner pain of knowing the young man's intelligence will be a sad loss for the hospital.

"That's Doc Smythe," the medic said upon recognising

Charles. "Best make sure he's alright miss... miss what?" he quizzed. "Not seen you at the hospital rounds." He paused. "Except for a few weeks ago. You look familiar..."

Charles groaned and grunted at the medic, "Can you stop your idle chit-chatting and put an end to this warm trickle on my face, please." He scowled at them both. "It probably needs a few stitches by the feel of it this side of the body."

Samantha nodded politely at the medic. "It's okay, I know what I'm doing."

She proceeded to open her bag and then froze, noticing the audience around her. Their eyes were peering relentlessly at the circus act – Sam's weird attire and the famous doctor.

The medic was twitchy and raised himself to his full stature, rebuking the prowling eyes.

In the background, the twittering of folks continued against the drumming of the outside world. Some sat and played cards. Some women had brought baskets containing darning kits, small pieces of cake, a little glass bottle of water, and prayer beads.

One man, who probably was a butcher, was arguing with a young black youth. The boy was probably about thirteen years old. The big man stood a few inches taller than the youth, booming in rage. He called him a useless nigger and proceeded to beat the boy about the head. The sergeant stepped in and told the butcher that the boy could be used as a runner. The radio had failed, and they were in need of information about the raid. The sergeant spoke firmly to the young lad. He requested his assistance and offered the use of a bicycle to aid his speed. The youth, not wanting to be in his employer's presence and be blamed for something his employer had done, accepted a far greater challenge. The sergeant took the boy to the radio operator and typed out a request despatch. The boy nodded and tripped past Sam.

Two women sat gossiping about the scene they had just witnessed and then proceeded to make rude comments about Sam's clothing. "Have you seen anything like that?"

"Oh no, Doris. Looks like a right harlot."

"No dignity in that. It doesn't leave a lot to the imagination."

"That be that young surgeon at the hospital. He should be a shamed of himself, associating with that sort of female."

"Can't call her a lady or a woman. More like a dog."

Then they giggled.

"I don't think she has something to do with the government. Is she Jewish? They dress funny. No wonder."

A voice from behind them hushed them to stop gossiping. It said gossiping costs lives and it's none of their business what people wear in this time of hardship.

The room was now filled with lots of tutting noises.

"How's the pain inside you head?" Samantha asked Charles.

"It only feels like the bomb landed on my head and not the factory," he grumbled. "Bloody awful, it's making me feel sick."

Samantha drew her bag close between them to grab something from inside it. Charles leaned forward to whisper to her, "Be careful opening that in here," his eyes flicking down to the leather bag. "I have seen the contents, and you have some unusual items that have to say in there.

They could cause concern, alarm, or possibly danger to you or me."

Needlessly, Sam continued with caution and rummaged around in it, churning the contents, making clanging and gangling sounds. She found what she needed without looking down inside the bag.

"This will kick any pain into oblivion." She smiled gently at him, handing him a strip pack of pain killers. He looked bemused. "Take two of them, and in about twenty minutes you be lucky to feel your legs." She smiled wryly. "It's an opium-based product," she continued, unsettled by the admission of have it. "It's prescription-only. The pain in my hand was so great that this was the only thing that touched it." He handled the blister pack curiously. "Here," she said, leaning a bit closer and popping two out into his hand.

"Amazing," he gasped. "Are you serious about the pain?"

She dabbed his head with a clean tissue from her bag. She reassured him, "twenty minutes, max. No pain."

He smiled at her reassurance and the gentle dabbing at the gash on his head.

"I meant your hand," he snorted in gaff laughter.

He then cupped his hand and dumped the pills into his mouth, swallowed hard, and then grinned at her.

"You want some water with that?" she asked as he swallowed. He shook his head.

"Mmm, stitches, aye," she remarked. "I might have something better," she pondered. "Staples or glue," she thought.

Then it dawned on her again: the reality check. She let

out a big sigh and dropped her gaze to the floor. Charles was gently squeezed her elbow, pulling her gaze back to him. "I have your suture kit in my bag." She patted the bag, blowing her cheeks out. "It's been a long time since I've done needle work."

Charles looked puzzled. "A nurse," he said, "that cannot suture?"

She continued whilst retrieving another item from the bag. "There are other methods available now other than using a needle and thread." She felt uncomfortable trying to explain her comments but continued to open the wooden box. "It's difficult to explain. Best leave it there."

Charles pointed at the correct thread and hook. She proceeded to clean the wound with the iodine from his Gladstone, staining his skin yellow. She removed the lodged shards of glass from the wound. He hissed through his teeth but remained still as she worked.

It was not a bad job. She was quite proud of her handiwork and smiled sweetly at him, giving a gentle laugh as she cast the last stitch. "Seven in total," she announced. "You have been really good; you have a sweetie now!" she jollied.

His response was now more promising that the pain relief was kicking in. The signs of a possible concussion were diminishing.

He smiled up into Sam's eyes, "Am I dead, or are you an angel?" he asked.

Sam hushed him. "You'll be fine now." She dabbed his brow.

"How bad is it?"

"It's better than having no head," Sam gave an

apprehensive laugh. "Any pain anywhere else?" Charles shook his head slowly.

When she was finished, she sat down next to him and said, "Good as new," with a big grin on her face.

"Perhaps you could put your newfound talents to use." He smiled and pointed behind her to a young boy whose leg was bleeding heavily from below the knee, a cut caused by flying debris.

"Be discreet," he warned, "paranoia reins in these times."

Sam now felt very self-conscious of all the eyes that had been observing them. She smiled nervously at the grubby child who seemed to have church candles for snot hanging from his nostrils and was so intrigued with the two of them. The boy proceeded to retrieve a large bogey from his left nostril and then gently roll it about between his finger and thumb before popping it into his mouth as a snack. Sam beckoned him over to get a better view of the wound. The boy's older sister appeared from behind him and enquired what was happening.

"What are you doing?" she asked with a broad cockney accent.

Charles spoke, "It appears that this young man has a laceration that needs attending too. What is your name, young lady?"

"What are you, some sort of doctor?" her words accused.

"Only one of the best!" Sam piped in, chastising the girl. "Mind what you say to the good doctor."

"Beg pardon, sir. There are so many strange things happening of late. All those Nazi spies and sorts bombing us and all."

"It's all right," Charles soothed. "Tell me what happened to this young fellow. What's your name, son?"

"I'm William. This is my sister, Roberta." The boy sniffed and pointed his bogey finger at the young lady.

"Where's your mum?" Sam enquired.

"You're dressed funny. Are you from the circus?" the boy replied, now staring at Sam's bright red boots. The girl gave him a sharp tap of reprimand.

"Our mother died two weeks ago of dysentery, thanks to those Nazi bastards blowing a hole in the water systems." The boy now gave a sharp tap back to his sister.

"Now, young William, what happened to your leg?" Charles beckoned him closer to get an examination of the wound. "Could you clean up the wound, please, nurse," Charles demanded from Sam. Sam looked up into his eyes, startled at the recognition of her profession. He winked at her and gave a wry smile. She pulled out a few more Mediwipes and began cleaning away the dirt. There were splinters of glass in the middle of the wound.

Charles pulled out the tweezers from his bag, but before he could reach over Sam's shoulder to pull out the debris, she applied a spray across the wound. He heisted, giving a curious look to Sam. She winked back, whispering, "Local anaesthetic." He nodded knowingly. The boy hissed through his teeth at the stinging sensation and then looked into Sam's eyes.

"It's stopped hurting." He smiled.

"That's good." She smiled softly. "Now you need to look away whilst the doctor cleans up the cut."

The boy shook his head. "I want to see what he does!" he protested.

"Very well," Charles smiled. "You best sit down though. I can't have you wriggling like a worm."

The boy sat on Sam's lap, and his sister held his hand.

The boy was cleaned and stitched up in no time, with Elastoplasts to cover the neat micro-needlework.

Before long, a queue of injured, sore people formed behind the two young kids. The girl helped coordinate them by who needed attention first.

The wildfire of gossip rang around the hall as the weirdly attired nurse bandaged up the injured.

Charles had just finished reforming some torn fingers when a blistering scream of help echoed from across the room. He was up on his feet quickly, a little unsteady at first with the effect of the opiates, and he sprinted past the forming queue. Sam gathered the bags together and was quick in pursuit.

At the far end of the hall, discreetly hidden behind a curtain that the young medic had hung, a young woman was writhing around screaming a high-pitched, ear-piercing scream. She was swathed in bloodstained clothing and was wrapped in an old blanket that was drenched in fresh blood. She smelt of stale, old blood. She was in labour. Charles knelt down beside her writhing body and glanced quickly at the woman next to her. "How long?" he asked and searched for the young medic who couldn't be found.

The woman, pale and exhausted, shrugged her shoulders. "A day or so, perhaps."

"What!" Samantha's sharp, fiery words spattered from behind Charles. "You don't know how long she's been in this state?"

Charles gave a rebuking look that Sam seemed to be impervious to. "Christ's sake, the baby could be dead or, or..." her words stammering in rage. "or, worse still, this young lady!" Sam pointed past Charles to the contorted, seething body. The woman continued to puff on her cigarette, flicking the ash near the young woman's writhing feet. The young girl groaned, panting in agony.

The older woman voice trembled. "I thought she would be through it now. We've been in here since yesterday. I can't move her. That young medical chap kept telling me to take her to the hospital, but she won't have it."

She dragged on her cigarette some more, flicking the ash again.

"I don't know what else we can do." She shrugged. "She has lost a bit of blood, but I did too, you know, when I had her. And it was a day or so before she popped out. I didn't think much of it, really." She smoked a bit more.

"Have the pain and contractions increased or are they about the same?" Charles gently requested, pushing down on the girl's stomach. He pulled out his stethoscope and listened to her rounded bump.

"It's hard to say," the woman continued. "I think her contractions have increased. She seems to be in more pain, I guess."

She puffed, blowing smoke rings. Charles felt the girl's lower abdomen, gently squeezing it with his fingertips. The young girl let out a high-pitched cry. He released the pressure. He looked at Sam and shook his eyes at her.

"Do you know if she is dilated in the birth canal?" he questioned again.

The woman shrugged. "How would I know that?"

"May I check?" he politely requested. The woman nodded, giving her cigarette another blast, flicking ash across Sam's hair.

Charles discreetly raised the covers to see if the baby was crowning, but it was not. The blood was congealed, with huge clots in the girl's vagina. He couldn't check for dilation because the girl writhed each time he attempted too. By the amount of blood lost, Charles knew she was bleeding internally. By the pain, he knew there was some form of blood clot. The girl fought for breath; her lungs were wheezing, coughing spots of blood. Charles shook his head again.

"She won't let me." His hands were stained with thickened red globules. The smell was retching. He wiped his hands discreetly on the blanket as he covered the pallid girl up.

The older woman dragged continually on her cigarette.

That was it. Sam lost it. "For fuck's sake!" Sam stood square to the older woman. She yanked the cigarette from the woman's mouth, hurling it to the floor and stamped on it. Sam brushed the ash from her hair. "Get the fuck out of my face." Sam's face was hardened and red.

Charles ignored the tirade and continued the assessment of his new patient. The older woman now put her hands on her hips, looking down at the crushed cigarette under Sam's right boot. She retorted, "No need to be rude. With a mouth like an open sewer... what are you, some sort of harlotwhat with a trap like that?"

"Get out of my way," Sam exclaimed, barging past to squat on the other side of the patient.

"Samantha," Charles firmly interjected, "it's a breech." His hands had been gently pushing the girl's tummy.

"Shit!" Sam squatted next Charles. Their eyes meet, knowingly. Sam, now back into her professional mode, looked back up to hard-faced woman.

"Breech, you say, doc?" the woman sighed.

"She is in grave danger. She has lost a lot of blood. I fear the baby may not still be alive. She has internal bleeding. I fear a blood clot." Charles spoke gently.

"What can you do, doc?" the woman asked wearily, and she shuffled through her handbag for cigarettes.

Sam looked towards the dirty floor and whispered to Charles, "We should do a C-section. Or try forceps. It's all messy. The poor girl has had massive blood loss already."

Charles's eyes glazed over with a deep sadness, and Sam knew what he was thinking. It could be too late for both mother and child. "If it were a dog..." he spoke in a gentle whisper. It was impossible. The girl was dying, and the baby was dead. She was bleeding to death. "Pass me my bag," he whispered. "The least I can do is make her comfortable." Charles's face was grim. His stitched forehead was furrowed, and his eyes were desperately sad as he gazed at the young girl.

Sam quizzed his expression, and in her heart she felt helpless and horrified. What was he going to do? What could he do? He stood up and faced the stony-faced woman. Taking his bag from Sam, who was holding the girls hand, he said, "There is nothing we can do." He peered down and then confidently spoke, "The baby is dead; there is no heart beat or movement. The girl has had massive blood loss and her internal organs are shutting down. I am sorry. I am very sorry." A tear formed in his eye, but it stayed as a glint.

The stony-faced woman screamed, "No!" She pawed her hands over her face, dropping her bag. "No! Do something. Do something," she kept screaming. Her body was shaking in despair. "How? Why? My little angel!" Her voice was shaking in hysteria. The medic came to assist. His face was grim as he scanned the blood loss and almost choked on the stale aroma.

He regarded Charles's sad expression knowingly.

"Christ," he exhausted, "I'll get a priest." He sprinted back across the hall to find the padre. Sam stood up, comforting the woman in a strong embrace to distract her from whatever Charles was going to do. He squatted back down beside the wheezing, sweaty, writhing body, and the girl let out another delirious cry. Charles acted quickly, closing his bag as fast as he had opened it. It only took seconds. He bolted upright, clutching his Gladstone and shoved past the two women, not looking back at the girl. He pawed a cloth to his forehead, pausing for Sam to follow. The padre appeared with the young medic, and the next act could move on.

Charles clutched Sam's elbow, leaning close into her, pressing his mouth against her ear. He whispered so small she barely heard his voice. He spoke firmly, "We must leave." The wailing began behind them. The older woman now clung to the padre, her tears wailing.

The padre began praying over the young girl, with the older woman still clinging to his long, black robes.

Charles's pace quickened as he barged past the gathering of onlookers around the dying girl. The sergeant was too distracted to notice them leave, except there was a brief chink of light flashing out into the deathly, droning sky.

## THE MIRROR

The metal groaning outside continued. The earth-shattering thunder of the antiaircraft guns sounded. There was an intense whistling of something sinister falling from the sky, bringing destruction and death.

Sam was now unsure of her new companion. What did he do? What did he have in his bag? He pointed towards the railway arches for shelter. She shook her head then spoke firmly to him. "The building, King George House, is still the same today as it was over sixty years ago. It had some small fire damage but was habitual. Why don't we go back there, away from people? And what did you do?" Her words tumbled senselessly.

His eyes meet her with rebuke. She was uneasy at prying but remembered his words, "If it was a dog". A spine-tingling cold embraced her core. His eyes pierced into her heart and her stomach somersaulted. Silence fell between them.

He pointed and continued to escort her towards the railway arches. The air filled with charring smoke and the smell of burnt brick, dust, and oil. The Messerschmitt filled the skies along with the flash and booming of the antiaircraft guns. But the bombs still came. Incendiaries tumbled, screeching Earthwards through the night sky, torching whatever was in their wake. Firefighters were attempting to extinguish the blazing wharfs. The flames danced high into the black sooty air, scorching and chastising the firemen.

Their pace quickened as the direction of the attack advanced back across the river towards London Bridge and Southwark. "Get under," Charles boomed, shoving Sam hard under the rail arch. A flash and hot scorching air singed the back of Charles's coat.

"Oh my god!" Sam cried out. Charles threw off his jacket

into a puddle to extinguish the heat and turned to where Sam was pointing.he picked up his coat cautiously shaking of the water.

The church hall had been directly hit. It was screaming; the fire took grip instantly. "Jesus," she screamed. "Jesus H."

Charles was trembling himself but pulled Sam close into him and held her tightly. Her body was jerking. She let out a cry of pity, devastation at the people lost, blown to pieces in a mad flash of a second. Her pitch didn't falter for a few moments; she didn't feel the tears that fell in her hair as Charles cupped her head under his chin. She didn't see the pain across his face and the guilt he felt within for the girl's life. The sickening knowing that in the morning light there would be families searching, torn apart from loved ones. There would be injuries and more poor conditions, undrinkable water and the sickening stench of death.

They stood cold and still, flanked by the embracing sanctuary of the arch. The air was moist from the gentle falling of spring rain. They waited not far from where the Clink was, wedged in an inner arch space that was destined to be a restaurant area in the future. The Earth trembled under the onslaught. The flashes and rumble continued. Trembling in cold rather than fear, she stopped sobbing. He released her with gentle words. "You spoke of the King House still remaining and undamaged?"

Sam nodded. "Well, the stairwell is a little more comfortable than here, wouldn't you say?"

She smiled a weary smile and sniffed in her tears. He handed his smudged, bloodied handkerchief for her to blow her nose on. She took it without questioning its hygiene.

"How is the noggin?" she enquired, lightly touching his brow.

He smiled confidently. "I've had worse headaches after a card game." He then gave a short chortle. "Come on, let's get out of this shit." It sounded funny to Sam's ears hearing him swear. His voice was so clinically clear, precise, haughty, but she was a fine one to criticise someone's bad language.

They took the shortcut through the back of the market, avoiding the wharf's blaze. They went around the church steps and dashed up onto the bridge, finding the entrance hallway.

They could hear a gathering of rescuers and firemen running towards the church hall shelter, freshly crushed and ablaze. Charles kept the two heading inwards.

# THE STAIRWELL

Flinging open the gallant doors, crashing them hard against the stops, they gave an inward hooray; they had made it. Charles scrutinized the entrance, squinting his eyes in the gloom, and gave a nod. He directed her towards the stairwell. It too was familiar to Sam, knowing where to perch.

The smoke had subsided and the air was breathable. The lower apartment was empty and the door had been jigged by looters. Charles carefully jostled open the door. No one inside. He tiptoed inside and within seconds retreated, holding ragged blankets and stained damp cushions. The top of the building billowed wearily with smoke from the burning wharf factory. Sam mentioned the need to relieve her bladder and bowel. Charles gestured her to be prompt, allowing her to enter the apartment and then to return to the cosy camp spot under the staircase. She fired up her torch and entered the blackness of the flat. She was quick, using tissue from her bag, and then she struggled at yanking the flush mechanism. She cussed, defeated by the cistern.

They huddled amidst the raid, wrapped warmly in the

tired ancient appearing blankets. Charles's eyes were soft and rounded, and he smiled at Sam in silence. From under his blanket, he produced a small, glinting bottle filled with an amber substance. Knowingly, Sam gratefully glugged her share of the bottle. Its liquid warmed her soul.

Charles quips about Sam's music contraption. Sam plugs it into its traveller's dock, picking a careful selection of tracks, skipping through Lenny Kravitz and Slipknot and finding Frank Sinatra, Neil Diamond, and Tom Jones.

Charles, intrigued with the complex sounds, fumbles with the device under Sam's instruction. Baffled, he blows out his cheeks and takes another glug from the bottle; they both giggle.

For a few moments, the roar of the thundering bombardment echoes through the hallway. Stressed voices call out urgently. They're too inaudible to hear the instruction they give. The tirade continues; the Earth trembles under the siege.

Charles turns to Sam. "So, my beautiful angel, where are you from?" She blushes at his charming words. "The accent is unfamiliar. West country? Ireland? Hell, Welsh, Belgium, Dutch?"

She giggles giddily under the influence of the strong whisky. She shakes her head.

"No. It's South African."

"African?"

She nods to confirm the answer. "Dutch colonist, Afrikaans, a real mix of the empire!" she retorts.

"Born there?" he asks.

She shakes her head. "No." She points at the floor.

"London, Hammersmith." She grins, giving a foul East End accent impression.

He laughs. "Why out in South Africa? And then back in London? Oh, and I do believe this is yours. I kept it everywhere I went. Sentimental, I guess. But please, it should be returned to its rightful owner." He smiles sweetly, fumbles in his jacket pocket, and pulls out the bracelet. He clasps it around he nearly healed hand. "There, much better." He winks.

Sam thanks him for all of his charm, but then her eyes drop from his wrinkled smile lines. "My parents," her words are trembling, "vets." She pauses, gasping and taking the bottle from his hand. "Big game reserve: lions, rhinos, you name it." Sam swallows a hard mouthful. "I was three when we went out. The sun, the birds, the heat, the fruit, the smells." She smiles. "It is wonderful... just be careful of the bloody baboons!" she remarks. "Nasty bastards. I saw a girl in my class get bit through the back of the leg. Nasty. It wanted her food; she was told not to carry it and leave it in the truck. Well, they just ambush you. We were all running around screaming. Their teeth huge are like knives. Got me too, we were both okay in the end. Hard lesson to learn. We had to be airlifted back to Johannesburg. They had to reconstruct the muscle." Charles nods knowingly.

"Well, it's okay being in Johan, but there are some nasty bandits as well, folks who will take whatever they can. Tribal conflict, gangs, – it's a bloody mess." She glugs from the bottle again, pausing as her lips tremble. "I was fifteen and..." Charles stares intensely at her, gently pulling the whisky bottle from her stitched hand. He clasps it gently. "Fifteen. I was with my cousin, Stephan. He was sent out there because he was trouble back home here in England. My uncle couldn't cope with his behaviour and thought that it would be good for him to live out on the farm with us, make him a man." She sniffs.

"We were at school in Johan, boarding; it was near the end of the summer term, and Stephan was sitting for his final A's. He is a few years older than me." Her words tumble softly. "His eyes... I won't forget his eyes, all red and puffed up. It looked like he had been stung. I was in my dorm; the girls, they loved Stephan. But when they saw him enter the room, instead of running and pawing at him, we all sat frozen. He paced around, rubbing his face. But his eyes... they held something terrible. The way he looked at me, a knowing look." She sniffs as a tear rolls down her cheek. Charles catches it with his thumb. He makes shushing sounds as he gently strokes her face. Then, drawing back her hand, she continues.

"Bandits," she remarks, "fucking bandits." Her head drops, sobbing lightly. "They came to the farm..." She shakes her head. "No chance... they torched the whole place. Killed all the stock, and my father had no chance of saving either of them... too many... crazy... my mother... my poor mother. What she endured before they burnt her alive. They tied up her naked, raped body, poured gasoline on her, and torched her." Sam is gasping to breathe. "They caught the bastards. They only ever found my father's head, a few miles from the farm." Charles's face is covered in horror. He takes a large slug from the bottle before handing it firmly back to her hand.

"Christ!" he rasps. "I thought I had a rough time over in France, with the first wave of the Germans storming across Europe."

Sam squints at him, remembering the raid outside. The doors are rattling under the explosions.

"France?" she whimpers, sniffing back her own self-pity.

"Yes, right by the bloody Somme." he blows out his cheeks. "My father was a British medical officer, a cousin I have to have say," he says haughtily, "of the great Victoria's family." He puffs out his chest proudly. "Of course, it's the duty to the country, to serve and lead by example." He laughs again. "Life, happy and fresh. Coffee... mmm."

He smiles. "French coffee, those baked fruit pies... oh, for one of those!" He gleans, throwing his head back in exaggeration. "My mother, wow, she can cook. And my sisters. But me, I got the genes of my father. I'm okay with slicing the roast, but I can't put flour and eggs together." He nudges Sam; she now giggles. "Well, my father, he was a right one." He puts his finger against his nose.

The Earth trembles from a close, loud explosion outside. They both pause in silence, with the faint rumble of the iPod hissing out Queen's "Don't Stop Me Now". He continues: "Flour and eggs! My father was posted to support the French surgeons and maintain an alliance with France, because there were murmurs from Germany of distain. He followed my mother for days, weeks, in and out the little sleepy village of Albert. He tried out his bad French on her. She pretended to misunderstand him just to tease him. They felt the same about each other. In the end, he enticed her with extravagant flowers." He laughs again. "My mother told me all sorts of funny things he got up to. Well, I was born first way back before the Germans came." He laughs. "Want to know how old I am?" He chuckles, nudging her again, laughing.

## THE MIRROR

"Well, he fell on the last days at the Somme during the summer of 1918. Shot by a German sniper trying to take over Albert. They succeeded, but only for a fleeting few months. The British had to blow up the Basialca to stop the Germans from using it as advantage point. The statue of the Madonna fell, and we believed then the war would end." He glugged at the whisky. "The ground was churned to blood, corpses lay in the fields, picked over by what wildlife was left after being scathed by the shelling. I witnessed the soldiers trooping through, blazed at the front and then returning to the village to die. They were either disfigured, missing limbs, or died from poor health. The villages were ravaged and torn by the monstrous death of their men and crop yields. Some nearly starved, and how hard of work it was to rebuild the homes and villages carved out by craters. I remember the blowing up of the mine at Lochnagar. The plume from the explosion went four thousand feet into the air. Apparently they used about sixty thousand pounds of ammonal explosives to detonate the mine. Mass graves were dug to stop the spread of infection and disease. It was terrible. We would be sent back to Amiens, far enough away from the threat of the front. But you could hear the torrid bombing, day and night. The thought of all those men being blown to shreds each time you heard the gunning and shelling.

"My mother was broken by my father's death. His body lay in some damp, dark shelled trench." His eyes brim. He sups the whisky again.

"I was pulled from France when I was six, to be educated at the King's expense. A royal blood line needed to be rescued and could not be left in the devastation of France and its famine. So I became a royal physician. I returned home to my mother and sisters each summer. And each time I returned to England, I was chastised for my accent. *Petite grenouille peut parler anglais? Il parle comment vas-tu appris!*" His words are flowing. "I very rarely speak French here in England. I can speak Latin too." He smirks.

"Your poor mother, loosing both men."

"She has strong shoulders. She is proud of me... despite the fact I cannot cook!" He smiles.

"Where and how is she now?"

"Knowing my mother and sisters, they will be cutting sleeping German throats when they sleep." He grins.

"How bad was it?" she questions, "the war?"

"Bloody." He bows his head. "I remember the troops, their limbs missing, endless blood flowing, and the smell, the sickness, and pain as they died. The women trying to save them. Stemming the blood flow. Agony to watch, dreadful. The pitted holes in the ground, the wallowing relentless trail if mud, rock, horses, fear... the fear in the soldiers' eyes. They knew nothing of what hell waited for them when they left the British shores or their Australian homes." He shakes his head in sorrow.

"Is that why you do so well in your surgery?" She requests the bottle. He nods, handing over the amber liquid.

"I had to do something. I knew I could do something. I wanted to change what I could – the healing process at least. I heard of a French pioneer surgeon from Paris who learnt to embroider. He began reconnecting blood vessels without tearing them. Amazingly mad, but it worked. Alexis Carrel. He received the Nobel prize in 1912 for the Carrel-Dakin method. I followed the surgeon and had the honour in Paris a few years back to be taught the technique. We became good friends, me assisting him in surgery. The odd thing was that he operated in black... always!" He turns her hand over, showing the tiny, neat stitches. She smiles. "Insistence endures. It's a shame Carrel was obsessed with the Nazi cause. I thought him a friend, but when he showed disdain to the Jewish faith, I stopped contact and returned back here to London."

"Neat job," she acknowledges, handing back the almost empty bottle.

"How long has it been since you have been back to France, and why did you come here to London?" Sam asks.

Charles puffed out his cheeks. "Well, I met a very good friend at the school. I was fifteen years old and a correspondent from the *Daily Mirror* was visiting. Funny-looking fellow, I thought, always wore a top hat. He joined in one of our card games, chugging on cigars and brought a bottle of whisky with him. He kept swearing in French." Charles laughs. "So I challenged his language, and we ended up having a conversation in French, taking the fun out of the other players." He glugs at the whisky. "He became one of my good friends." He smiles. "We ended up down in the village that night, chasing the maidens there. Well, what else do I need to explain?" He grins. "Ah, we had some fun," he sighs.

"He requested I come back to London from Paris about three years ago when he heard of the problems in Albert." He puffs out his cheeks and swigs the bottle, rolling the liquid around his mouth.

"What troubles?" Sam questioned gently.

"My fiancé... she was collecting wood out in the fields and never came home."

"Your fiancé?" Sam asks, astonished and hooked.

He nods. "She was lying with the basket in her hand. Just dead. Like life had been taken from her in an instant." He swigs. "Horrible, really. She was found in the late evening. No injuries, nothing. They seemed to think it was some sort of curse, a bad omen; such superstitions women have, no offence. I was too distraught to go back. I couldn't face her funeral; it hurt too much." His head lowers. "What could I have done? Nothing, and they seemed suspicious of me and my family. It was dreadful. They thought that by travelling back and forth to England, Paris, and through the Netherlands, I was carrying some sort illness or that I had done some deed to a gypsy. Ah, it's rubbish really. People need to learn to look at things more succinctly." He shook his head. "She was so young, so healthy, so strong and fit. No reason."

"It sounds like cardiac myopathy", Sam interjects, matter-of-factly. "It just happens to some people. It's difficult to detect until symptoms appear. Young rugby players or athletes die on the track or field. If it's sudden cardiac death, the person doesn't even know about it; they shut down instantly, fatally, with resuscitation impossible. The heart is so damaged, the ventricles can be thickened, and subendocardial fibrosis can manifest itself. It can be caused by a faulty gene issue. Born with it, undetected." Sam continues to explain. "Even if you were there, there would be very little, if anything thing, you could have done. I'm sorry."

Silence falls between them. The clattering and booming of the guns and rattle of the night raid shake the walls.

Charles speaks in a whisper "A gene fault?"

"Yes, your make-up DNA. It's amazing how many aliments we can now detect through a faulty gene. Cancer, Down's syndrome, arthritis, technology has even gone into developing a resistance against the HIV virus."

Charles scowls quizzically at her. "So, the gene can be detected? And altered?"

"Well, for instance, cystic fibrosis can be found in an unborn foetus. And if the fault is there and the child will probably be born with the disease, the mother can choose to abort the foetus. Likewise with Down's."

Charles's face looks horrified at the idea of aborting an unborn child.

Sam shrugs. "It happens. But you can be tested for it to see if you're a carrier. And if your partner is also a carrier, there's a higher risk of having a child with the condition. But a lot of people don't bother."

"Tell me more about this DNA gene."

"Oh, it's really for big brains. Two men named James D. Watson and Francis Crick discovered the double helix – a chain or alignment of links that makes us who we are. Me, a girl with blue eyes; you, a man with dark hair and amber eyes. It's simple, really," she explains tiredly.

"Intriguing." Charles puts down the bottle and holds her hand. "You're freezing." He wraps the blanket a little tighter around her, cuddling her close to him for warmth.

"Try getting some sleep. Not meaning to be rude." He clears his throat. "It will be a busy day tomorrow." He looks skyward. "With the sounds of the wreckage out there, it will be hectic at the office." He plonks a cushion onto his lap, and Sam snuggles up to him, allowing him to fiddle with her long golden locks, twirling them whilst she drifts away under the heavy influence of the whisky. For a fleeting moment, she thinks she can hear Simon's voice calling her.

"I have some answers now," Charles whispers sadly. "Sleep well, little angel."

He sits adrift in thought, fiddling with the iPod.

# THE MEDIUM

"What the hell do you mean she vanished!" Simon stormed over the phone at Jenny. "You interfering cow! I told you to stay out of it with your bloody hocus-pocus shite."

"Simon..." Jenny wept, "it was nothing to do with us. Honest."

"Bullshit," he raged.

"We only sat down, and then it all happened."

"Bollocks, Jenny. You're a bad liar."

"Just come over, Simon, please?" she pleaded.

"I will be five minutes. Is the witch still there?"

"Do you want her to leave?" she asked.

"No!" he bellowed. "I want to talk to her." He hung up.

Jenny's eyes were red and sobbing. She flicked the phone onto the table. The medium, still pallid, spoke softly, "She is with him."

Jenny broke. "Oh, shut up. It's your fault," she blasted.

The medium shook her head. "No, no, it's the fate of the gods and the trueness of the heart. The intertwining of worlds does happen, but it's so rarely seen or logged in such perfection."

"What the fuck are you talking about?" Jenny asked, feeling frustrated in dismay.

"Destiny." She nodded kindly, ignoring the harsh words. "Destiny to help us be who we are today. There is a purpose to fight against the evils of the human heart. The unkindness that we can become or embrace." She wiggled her finger. "Look around you today. So many are ungrateful; so many find comfort in food; so many do not understand themselves and the true human heart and its good spirit." Jenny, now attentive, sat down opposite the medium.

"Sometimes the angels will come and gather souls to place them where they can mend, where holes have come. This will forward the trueness of the heart as two souls are joined in the endless battle against divine evil and atrociousness." She nodded and fell back into silence, concentrating.

A loud rapping came from the door. Simon.

Jenny tentatively paced the hallway, took in a deep breath, and unfastened the heavy oak door. Simon heaved the door almost off its hinges and marched in towards the main seating area, and his glare fell onto the medium, who still sat in silence.

He opened his mouth to blast cruel words but was stunned by what he felt. A curious, cold, eerie sensation crept over him from his stomach to his skin. He smelt the burning acrid tar and could hear the distant pounding and droning outside. He closed his mouth and pounced forwards to the balcony. He pitched the windows open and swore he could hear the crunching of broken glass beneath his feet.

He spun on his heels and then spoke in spiked remarks. "What trickery is this?"

The medium gazed softly into his ferocious, angry eyes. "You fight it, don't you?"

"What are you speaking of? What have you done here?"

"Yes, you fight it… yet it is so strong in you." She stood up, all four feet five of her. Her clothes jangled and sparkled, and she moved in small gestures. "You fear it… so you should. Such power."

Simon lost his patience. "Stop sounding like bloody Yoda and tell me what you did!"

"Not I… she did."

"What!"

"She did. They both did." She nodded.

Jenny interpreted. "She says that two souls can find each other for the good of all."

They both pointed towards the kitchen where the bouquet of flowers was placed. Simon stormed into the kitchen and viewed the flowers. Simon, bemused, picked up the yellowed card and immediately recognised the handwriting. He pushed the card firmly down into his back pocket. He returned to the main living area, red-faced and pondering.

"Oh, don't give me that Mills and Boon shite, Jenny. I warned you not to mess with this shite; it's bloody dangerous." He scorned her. "Well, rag a bag, where the bloody hell is my friend Sammy?" he demanded, now flashing the card.

The medium smiled gently. "She is here in the building somewhere, but she is not here with us."

"Yes, I have perfect eyesight. Where?"

"A question of when," she replied.

Suddenly, the same sensation crept over him. He peered into the mirror and blurted out, "That fucking diary." He snapped his fingers, crushing the card hard in his palm.

"Come on, rag a bag and metal Mickey, we're off to the hospital. And you, metal Mickey, better come up with a good scam to get us in the library." He hooked hold of the medium and shoved Jenny towards the door.

# THE HOSPITAL

For a brief moment, through the haze of alcohol and Charles's Samson tobacco roll ups and probable use of his hidden pipe and stash of opium, Sam was sure as she drifted that she heard Simon's voice ringing through the hallway. Complaining as usual, stabbing hurtful comments about Jenny's facial piercing and jabbering on about the diary.

Charles thought better of rummaging in Sam's bag. He was intrigued as to what else she had stashed in it, but he continued puffing on his pipe. He too drifted into a light slumber, despite the echoes of the firemen battling with the night's blazes.

The sirens wailed again, the pitch different to give an all-clear. Wearily, they pushed back the covers and rose to their feet, rubbing their eyes, and paced to the entrance. The doors clanged opened, and the dim light of dawn spread across the swirl of smoke and the Thames. The firemen were still battling the blaze of the warehouse and wharfs. Gauged holes of shrapnel were strewn across the road and bridge; various sounds of command and reassurance echoed as the

German planes ceased across the dawn horizon, fading past Tower Bridge. The air was thick with the aroma of cordite dust, and burning hot brick and the sound of crackling wood, steel, and iron hissing.

They stood holding each other on the bridge, viewing the last wave of the bombers into the sunrise. The guns were silent; an eerie reprieve crept over London. She felt in her heart something so powerful: the sense of becoming. Her bag buzzed with the sound of her iPod through mobile dock and speakers; the song was by Procol Harem. "Odd," she thought, "why would it do that? Not all through the night unless someone had been fiddling with it." She felt odd, out of place, surreal. The planes were now dim in the skyline and the black smoke of their wake billowed in the crackling of fire. A small child was crying in the distance. Her heart sank, thinking and knowing of the ill-fated people, good and frightened in the church hall.

A small ginger cat appeared, rubbing happily around the pair's legs. It was gently caressing its head and chin on the backs of their legs with a soft, rumbling purr of pure pleasure to have human company again. Sam reached down to the cat's direction. "It's in really good shape," she commented to Charles. "I love cats; they're so intelligent." She gave it a good stroke and tickle around its chin and ears. Charles smiled and did the same.

They began walking towards the market with the cat weaving between their legs. "Better see what the hospital needs us for... and if it's still there." Wearily, he sighs.

"This little fellow knows a few hidey holes. Keep up the good work with the rats." He pats the cat's head. "Tram lines seem to have stayed in not too bad of shape. They will be rumbling back up." He pointed. "Mind your step." He lifts Sam's elbow so she doesn't trip on the rail.

Two ladies emerge from a house by the bridge. They too are weary and blurry-eyed. Charles waves at them from across the street and calls to see if they need help. They reply no. Then, as he stops to chat to the ladies, the cat darts away from the pair. He scouts and bounds down the steps into Green Dragon court by the cathedral, bounding towards the market under the arches, gone like a bolt of lightening.

Charles comes over coldly and quick-thinking. He pushes Sam down the steps behind the cat. She looks hurt and confused as her knees smash hard against the granite. Suddenly, there is a massive boom. The air is vacuumed; empty compression strains their lungs and pricks their skin. The whole Earth shudders. Then, just as quickly, the air fills with projectiles of brick, wood, and something that appears to be human at one time. Debris showers above their heads, the fresh spattering of the two now-dead women.

Sam screams out, crouching on her knees with her hands over her head. Charles is squatted down beside her, embracing her tightly. The hail finishes in milliseconds. Parts fall behind them onto the steps and rail like mad artwork from the Tate Modern. Some of it appears to be part of a butcher's offal section; one piece is defiantly a hand.

Sam's eyes question, terrified. Charles whispers, "Butterfly."

Sam shakes her head; she doesn't understand what he means but is too unnerved to enquire. Charles gingerly rises to his wobbly feet and beckons Sam to do soothe same. After a few seconds, he peers through the iron rail at the top of the stairs. Carefully, they tread. But the grit and dross is strewn. Her knees hurt and are bruised from being bashed on the hard steps. Her lungs and skin were singed.

They cautiously approach the top of the steep steps, confounded by the freshly mashed rubble. The bodies of the women are fused and spattered amongst the piles of debris. Blood and flesh were projected everywhere; the stench of partly charred human flesh is rank. Sam swallows hard but can't contain the bile and vomits violently, just missing her boots. Charles stands stone-faced at the commotion, as if he had seen it a hundred times before. He caresses his hand down Sam's back in complete empathy. Firemen are running towards them from the wharf; luckily they were too far around the corner to be caught in the blast. One man leaps across the boulders, calling to the pair.

Charles replies they are fine, but the two are not. He tells the fireman their names. Sam looks into the stoniness of Charles's face as he addresses the fireman. He continues to announce that they were volunteers at the hospital, helping bomb victims. The fireman tips his tin hat and allows the pair to continue, but with caution, of course. Charles explains where they're heading and then asks about casualties. The fireman shakes his head but then is distracted by the call of his team. There is no fire where the houses once stood, just rubble and detritus.

They move forward a few paces, slowly regaining their composure. Sam now felt the acid aftertaste of bile burning her throat. She makes small throat-clearing noises. Charles pulls the amber bottle from his bag and offers Sam to sip it. She does so willingly and is grateful to clear the bile and feel the liquid's strange warming comfort.

Charles surveys the buildings and his heart sinks; the side windows of King George House have been blown in by the pressure of the blast. He is now homeless. He sighs. But he's grateful in his heart for the life still coursing through his veins.

The cat reappears some yards ahead, bouncing back towards the pair. Once again, he chaperones them for a few hundred yards, weaving between their legs, before being distracted by the rustling of a gutter.

The railway bridge had been completely missed, but the line was broken further down where the antiaircraft post had been two nights previously. Prudently, it had moved in anticipation of the attack.

They crossed over the High Street, stepping over bits of strewn brick and dangling cables from the overhead tram lines. Sam knew where she was, but it was too different. The houses in St Thomas Street did not exist; they were just chewed up bits of brick wall. It was as if some giant had spat it out in distaste. They didn't speak, but Charles clutched her hand on the road crossing and then pulled her tightly to his side and wrapped his arm around her middle. The hospital was not in bad shape; the main courtyard was free of debris and was an easy thoroughfare. Part of the maze wing had been hit, and there was a busy entourage of rescuers, firefighters, ARPs, and anyone that could pull or move and keep their head from panic. Charles opened the double doors and ushered Sam through them first. Sam had been in the building many times, but it was stunning to see it being used as a general ward and clinic. She smiled softly at the approaching nurse. The uniform was grandiose; the headdress was starched white and curved, almost flapping as the nurse quickened her short march to greet the pair. Sam almost gasped as the nurse spoke; it sounded familiar and kind.

"Good morning, doctor. Glad to see you in one piece. And Miss..." the accent was a mix of Irish with a spattering of Polish. "What happened to your head? And whose neat handiwork is that?" Charles ran his hand along the stitches on his forehead and gave a wry smile. He tilted his head towards Sam, quickly rolling his eyes. The nurse nodded knowingly.

"How's that hand of yours doing, miss?" she gently enquired, putting her hand forward for Sam to surrender the injured part to.

"It's healing rather well, thank you." She showed the nurse the faint scarring.

"Better keep it clean, that sure handiwork of our good doctor here." She gave a wink at Charles, who had released Sam from his clutch and was modestly blushing.

"Oh Sister, what happened to maze wing?" Charles quickly changed the subject.

"Oh, well..." The sister paused. "It was one of those awful butterflies. It missed the bridge and, boom, got us." She shook her head, making the starched bonnet flap again. "We have a few survivors. Well, what's left of them, poor souls." She looked up into the doctor's eyes. "Don't think there is much you can do, such blood loss. I don't rate their chances."

"How many?" His face was now stone.

# THE MIRROR

"Twenty, maybe thirty. Some psychiatric, some wounded soldiers, a real mix." The nurse choked back the tears in her eyes. "I... I..."

"We can only do what we can, Eunice." His words were gentle. She sniffed and nodded. "We have an excellent set of new hands that can be put to use." He presented Sam. "That is, of course, if you don't mind, Samantha."

"Pretty name," the sister replied.

Sam nodded; she informs them both that she would do what was needed. Her accent was rapidly switching from London English to Afrikaans. The sister frowned at the accent. Charles addressed it: "A little like you, Eunice. A mixed upbringing."

Sam interjected. "My father travelled and work around Europe and Africa. I spent many years in Africa," she explained.

"Ah, we are something alike, then," Sister Eunice excitedly replied. "Better come this way and get the two of you cleaned and ready for action." Her manner was friendly and warm. She ushered them along the corridor and into a more private room with a wash basin, toilet, freshly starched towels, and a neatly tucked-up starched iron-framed bed.

Charles smiled. "My room at the inn."

"Would you be needing a change of clothing, doctor?" Eunice asked.

He nodded. "The usual, please."

They both looked at Sam's attire. Sam looked at herself and agreed to put on a uniform. She cocked her head and recalled the nurse. "Thank you for looking after me," she informed her gently, "and thank you, doctor. My hand would have been permanently damaged if not for your handiwork."

They both smiled appreciatively at Sam. Nurse Eunice informed them she would back in a few minutes with a change of attire and left.

"My eyes are killing me!" Sam exclaimed. She headed for the sink and mirror.

"What's wrong with them?" Charles quizzed

"My lenses were in way too long. I need to rest them. Feel like they have sand in them ,so dry " She proceeded to wash her hands and dried them on the starched linen. She took one lens out, but then before she could pinch out the other, Charles snatched her hand away from her eye, inquisitively. He opened her hand to view the scrunched lens.

"Oh, sorry," she said, knowing that it could look a bit squeamish for some observers.

"No, it's okay," he continued. "I want to see how they work." He was close to her personal space; his face was almost pressed against hers as his eyes beeded into hers .

"See." She stroked her finger across the lens, making it move, and then she released it to bounce back into its resting place across the cornea.

"Amazing. Intriguing," he gasped, breathing onto her face.

"And then..." she dragged the other lens down off the cornea and pinched it out, handing the perfect domed lens into his hand. His eyes were wide with delight and intrigue. He pulled back a few feet, out of her space. He peered down at the tiny, clear, floppy plastic and poked it with his finger, shaking his head in wonderment.

A rap at the door disturbed any further instruction.

Eunice came in and handed them each a bundle of

neatly presses starched clothing. "Chop chop... work to be done! I will be back with some tea and breakfast." She turned on her heels and firmly closed the door.

"How far can you see?"

"With or without the lenses?"

"Without."

"Oh, probably about 15 centimetres." she shrugged.

"Really? To about here?" He pushed his face close in again, and Sam was unsettled with his action, nudging his shoulder away.

His words were embarrassed. "Sorry, I did not mean to make you feel uncomfortable."

He put his fresh linens onto the bed. "I will wait outside while you change," he stammered. "Call me when I can come in. Don't be too long, we have the needy to attend to." He fumbled the edges of the linens and, without any eye contact, promptly left the room.

Sam, bemused at what had just happened, unfolded the uniform curiously and looked at the hefty clogged shoes. She looked around the sparse chamber, and quickly changed. Her eyes were too blurry and too sore for the lenses, so she fumbled in her bag for her eyeglasses. She viewed herself in the mirror before beckoning to the doctor. She decided that the rimless spectacles were out of place and placed them in the pocket of the nurse's scratchy attire.

She then waited outside.

When he was clad in his doctor's whites, he allowed her re-entrance.

"Do you have spectacles?" he pried.

Sam fumbled in her pocket. "They look odd." She shook her head as she positioned the spectacles.

"Whoa, hey." He grinned. "They're fabulous. But you need to wear them; we can't have you stepping on something!" She nodded at his instruction. "Just tell them they're new and experimental if anyone asks." He grinned , winking at her.

Self-conscious and awkward, followed him through the corridor into the hospital.

She whispered to him as he strode forward, "How long was I here before?"

"Three weeks." His eyes were focused ahead.

"Why did you keep me sedated?"

His pace stopped, and he turned his heel towards her. "Listen," he addressed her gently, putting his hand against his ear. They both stood silently. Her heart thumped at the wailing, the cries for help, the shuffle outside of the firemen, the racing neighbours. "Every day, the same din," he continued. "You were having screaming fits and terrible nightmares. You spoke uncontrollable gibberish." He shrugged his shoulders. "I had no choice, really."

"What kind of nightmares?" she urged him.

"They did not make sense. You were speaking gibberish. You appeared to be fighting something."

"Oh." She blushed. "It's Afrikaans, actually... the language."

He tilted his head. "Really?" he asked in bemusement. "What were you fighting?"

"I was attacked when I was eight by a baboon." She paused, turning to show him the back of her leg. She pointed. "That's where it sunk its teeth into my calf muscle," showing him the scar. "I hate monkeys... and if anyone suggests to me that we evolved from them...." She wrangled her fist.

"I am so sorry," he sympathised

"It's not your fault, is it?" She beamed. "Bastard things." She spun back and marched confidently forward. He scratched his head, absorbing the information, and then hotly pursued her.

"Afrikaans?" he quizzed.

She nodded. "If you're a good boy, I will teach you some later," she teased.

"Put that magic bag of yours in one the doctor's Gladstones, and hide it under one of the the beds in the doctors quarters. They'll think it's mine and wont dare touch it." He pointed towards an alcove "down there on the right. The one with the large plaque on it . Is mine" he smiled

Sam quickly responded to his request and within a moment she was back with the doctor heading towards the Maze wing.

\* \* \*

Simon was ranting all the way from King George House to the hospital. He kept making puns to Jenny, and the medium slinked alongside them, trying to be invisible.

"You got a mobile?" Jenny bleated to Simon.

"Of course I have, dummy. You phoned me on it!" he spat.

"My battery is dead. Can I borrow yours?" she gently enquired. Simon spun on his heels. Hands on hips, he blew out his cheeks in preparation of a verbal attack. "I can ring Stephan, he can get us in," s her word stacato. "You know I am right, right?" She nodded.

"Stephan," thought Simon, "any chance...?"

He thrust his phone into Jenny's hand. "Don't gabble on it too much, just get the hunkster down here, ASAP!" Jenny grinned at Simon's new excitement for the new number she was plugging into his phone.

Rossini piped up. "What is this diary?" Her words flowed with intrigued. Simon flapped at her, ignoring her question. He was too interested in Jenny's conversation with Stephan.

"The diary..." Jenny began as she flicked off the phone, but Simon immediately butted in.

"Well, Metallica?"

"Oh, he will be here in few moments. We need to meet him by the tower entrance." Jenny made no eye contact. She focused on the medium.

"Well, that's fine!" Simon flounced and sauntered onward towards the hospital entrance.

"The diary, you'll see." She grinned at the medium.

They paused by the tower entrance, a little bedraggled by the falling fine rain. Stephan arrived with a big fat grin on his face. "What's up, guys?He bemused them Why so late and why so urgent?" He looked around at the strange entourage. "Where's Sammy?" he quizzed

"Can we get inside, please? And then, erm, we will explain."

Stephan scratched his head but trustingly agreed. They dodged the security guys giving them an excuse of late night research, and flashing their identity cards to prove all above board.

They approached the library; its foreboding darkness gave them all a spine shudder. Simon spoke first as Stephan unlocked the door and gave the security pass code. "It's much easier to explain if I show you."

Stephan cocked his head. "Show me what?" he smerked.

He pondered whether this was turning into something distasteful.

Simon was through the barrier and leapt over the clerk's desk t in a truly magnificent single bound, to find the diary stashed in Sam's reserved pigeon hole. Jenny threw on her torch and proceeded to the back of the library. Its beam shifting to and fro across the study desks and array of book shelves. Stephan stood in the entrance with the squat medium behind him both with the appearance of bewildered game show guests.

Simon beckoned them both in. Jenny found an angle lamp and set up the desk. They all held their breath as Simon planted the diary down.

"This is where Sammy is," he announced. "Let's find her."

"What?" chortled Stephan. The three others nodded. "You've gone mad!"

"Perhaps. We do not know how the whole truth of the universe and how it functions . We are just small, and who knows what it wants from us," Rossini interjected with her creepy riddles .

Simon opened the leather-bound book. As he read aloud, Stephan was aghast.

> My fair maiden is beside me. She is an angel to those around us. Her strength is so willing and never once has she complained of the drudgery that is upon us in these hard times. I know by her eyes that some of what she views is disturbing. Any man would have vomited at the explosion of

the Glenister sister's house. Those two ladies were a sad loss to the world, with their gentle, kind spirit of helping others. Samantha, although shaken, stands back on her feet to carry on in the duty that calls us all.

The hospital was hit in the maze wing and Sister Eunice beckons for extra help. Of course, we all chipper along. The unit was holding about twenty-five patients, some from the psychiatric ward and others so poor in health they were in fits of madness from fever. I pray that Fleming's new cure will be available to us sooner rather than later. My beautiful angel shows me a new correction for eyesight, something bizarre and wonderful: a lens that sits on top of the cornea, like a glove, purposely made. However, the night's bombings and the ashen air have made her eyes too sore to wear the lenses. She has the most glamorous spectacles and causes quite a stir with them. Sister Eunice informs us of the atrocities ahead and the firemen wouldn't let her near the wing at first because the sight was so terrible. It was indeed.

We could hear some moans from the mashed rubble and screams of help.

Parts of patients bodies were strewn across the debris; blood splattered as far as the eye could see. The smell was overwhelming, and the fair maiden, I noticed, choked back the bile. I too had to hold fast and think past my own churning. We had not eaten much. Eunice gave us tea and some bread and drippings whilst we changed into our meds.

The food stayed lodged in both our stomachs, thankfully.

One of the nurses was pulled from the pile; however, she had sadly lost the lower part of her legs. The blood loss was so great that she died some two hours later, the pain she endured as her body ebbed away from this universe. Eunice was deeply upset; she was a good friend of hers, and she sat and kept her company whilst she passed.

We spent the day cleaning the building and sterilising equipment, and I attempted several surgical procedures. One fellow had a lucky escape. My angel, Samantha, found him wedged between two collapsed walls. A pocket, she called it. He had lost several digits, including his thumb; he had a gashed arm that needed about thirty stitches. The rest of him was just shaken up. Samantha informs me, ingeniously, about transplanting a toe to his hand to use as a thumb. My concern is the course of infection. But if Fleming is right, it could be a possibility.

Stephan rubs his eyes. "Coincidence!" he barks. "You guys are nuts." He stood to his feet to leave.

Simon flicks back the pages to show the evidence. Rossini is astounded.

Stephan re-seated himself making the chair squeak ,he instructed Simon to continue to read.

"Carry on, Simon," Stephan orders, intently watching the faces of everyone.

> Our day is long, but at last we can rest. The medical officer that helped us in the shelter has appeared. We are glad of his assistance and to see him alive.
>
> He informed me that the young woman that died in the shelter that night was the sad reason for his narrow escape. The priest and he had taken her body into the church to lay it to rest and to pray for mercy on our souls. He asked me what I did, but I told him nothing of the injection.
>
> Samantha embraces him, and I feel a little twinge of jealousy, hoping it was me in that hold.
>
> Eunice telephones ahead to her father's house across London to enquire if we can stay with them, because I am homeless at present. It is agreed. She has a big house and is always taking in refugees of the raids. We are glad to go there.
>
> As she leaves, giving directions to the route, the sirens go again. The guns start

# THE MIRROR

to rattle. It is still light out, and the German planes have increased their confidence. We continue our ward rounds, checking to block out any escaping light. Our clothes are dirtied again, and Samantha insists on putting back on her very tight trousers. She informs me she feels more comfortable in them than the scratchy skirts. I oblige. We return to my humble doctor's room; she allows me to watch her open a foil and insert fresh lenses. She feels far happier. She complains about not having washed and smelling, but I tell her that there should be a warm bath at Eunice's parents' house. She teases me about when I saw her slumber in her bath. I guess I am red-faced to describe her beauty to her. She just smiles and then giggles, requesting I have my eyes checked out.

The phone rings, and Cyril Germane, the fire chief, tells me that a bus has been hit on the north side. A good surgeon is needed and along with extra hands at Forest Gate.

The young black boy is at the hospital entrance, and again he is embraced by the fair maiden. He has come to help assist the nurses if they need anything fetched or carried, as he no longer has an employer.

I call Sister Blackwell to employ the boy

in something useful and to keep a watch on the direction of the sky.

Samantha suggests we take one of the motorbikes, but I desist, informing her I dare not operate such a beast. She smiles, teasing me to get on the back, and kick-starts the Triumph. She pulls something from her bag of tricks and tells me to stick it in my ear and to sit close. The beast of a bike throbs with a deep, guttural sound. I sit tightly behind her; she fiddles with something in her bag, with the strap slung across her body. Suddenly, my ear fills with music – strange, giddy, pulsating pandemonium. I ask what it is. She grins over her shoulder and tells me to enjoy it, saying its one hell of a track to ride to in a raid on a Triumph. She unscrews the cap on the tank, checking the fuel shakes the bike, and then yells at me through the fracas above and the buzzing in my ear. I think she informs me to hold on tightly for the ride of my life. She opens the throttle, and we blast around the courtyard and hammer down St Thomas Street and up over London Bridge. Swaying and dodging the pot holes and strewn debris. The river is full of firefighting barges; they seem to be further up river where the raid is concentrated. My heart races; my arms tightly grip her waist, and I feel exhilarated and thrilled, almost to the point of something perverse. I cannot control the deep sensation, and I fear embarrassment. Her hair dances and billows around my face, and I have to bury my face into the small of her shoulders. I admit it is something a man cannot hold back, to be so tightly entwined with such an amazing creature, all woman. She still has the aroma of the light perfume, despite the foul work we have been engaged in. We dodge the gaping holes in the roads, the low flying shrapnel, and the heat from burning buildings. We are diverted on several occasions; she is a most excellent handler. My bag bumps around on the wired back basket, and I cling for dear life on the small saddle we are both perched on. A few heads turn to watch us rumbling along with a female driver and me grinning in wonderment.

We arrive at the scene in Forest Gate and my soul is stunned. We sit on the bike for moment, gawking at the carnage. The music is still hauntingly playing, and I remove the earpiece, subtly handing it to Sam. She switches off the music and then the Triumph. I dismount with rather shaky legs. She pulls the bike onto its kick stand . Cyril Demure approaches us.

"Glad you could get here, doc." His face

is pallid. "Never seen anything like it... poor souls."

"Any survive?" I enquire. Cyril shakes his head.

"Not from the bus, but some of the neighbouring houses and shops have a few injured in them, if you can help. If that's okay. Thanks, doc, for coming. " He tilts his tin hat. "I like your mode of transport," he says, winking at Samantha.

Samantha:

Sam's legs went, Like solid stone. It was a wonder she didn't fall off the bike. She clutched her bag tightly and withheld the acidic bile from spilling out of her mouth. She swallowed hard, but her throat kept wanting to let it up. She was more and more astonished at the devastation she was facing, but nothing prepared her for such a chaotic mess. The Routemaster bus (what was left of it) had its front end tipped down into a crater that was once road. The top deck was completely missing, and the downstairs passengers were still in their seats with their hands clasping their tickets, awaiting the ticket inspector. However, their bodies were ripped open from the torso upwards with all of their heads missing. The whole lot was decapitated in an instant. There was a stench of cordite and charred human flesh, and there was a thick treacle of blood spattered amongst the metal debris.

The bus had taken a direct hit. She searched beyond the scene curiously to see where the roof had been blown to. Fragments of metal, curled and twisted, were strewn from one side of the road to the other, imbedded into the surrounding buildings, mashing the remnants of the passengers into walls. The smell was intense: sulphur, broken sewers, and the horrid, acrid stench of burnt flesh and seeping blooded wounds. She trembled slightly, thanking the stars inside she was somehow alive. Weird and tremendous questions rose in her; she turned her head downwards to prevent her eyes from absorbing anymore of the horror. The sky continued to boom, fizzing with the evil of the incendiaries and explosives that were blasting the houses on the streets behind her. The firemen, struggling with the immense, snaking of hoses, were battling the furnaces.

For a few seconds, she was lost in her mind, but she quickly overcame the fainting sensation creeping up from the pit of her stomach. A conversation sparked next to her. Charles was assessing the scene with some fire chief. She couldn't remember his name. Charles's hand reached out and squeezed her shoulder as the fire chief sauntered back to the bus.

Charles spoke softly, "You look a little pale... you okay?" Sam nodded, unable to speak.

"Horrible, isn't it?" she murmured "How long? Why? Why are they doing this to us?" Her words became frantic. "These people have families, babies; what are those bastards doing? Why? Why the fuck are they slaughtering us?" Hysterical, she screamed her words. Her eyes were wide, mad. Her arms were flailing around. "Look at them, just look at them. Why did they deserve to be decapitated, slaughtered, killed? Murdering bastards. They hate. They hate. Murdering fucking bastards." Charles tried to grab her by the shoulders, but she was too highly agitated. She swung out of his grasp, still screaming. She doubled over with pained tears streaming across her face. "Murdering fucking bastards. Fuck. Fucking Nazi cunts."

The fire chief turned to witness Charles slap Sam across the cheek. Her faced twinged and turned pink; her mouth was open in stunned silence. Charles grabbed her by the shoulders and pulled her into his embrace. She collapsed into his arms, sobbing hard and snorting as her nose dripped. Her whole body jerked. Her sobs were muffled by his chest. It was some minutes before Charles could safely release her. Her eyes were red, her face was streamed with black lines from her makeup. She wiped her nose on a tissue she found crumpled up in her jeans pocket. "I'm sorry," she whimpered.

"I'm sorry too. Does it hurt?" His hands were gentle. He touched her pink cheek.

"A little. It's okay." She sniffed. " I was really mad... I've never felt like that... only when..." She paused and the sobs welled up again. This time they were from the painful memory. She realised where her reaction had come from. She carried the pain with her, buried deep down, hidden, forgotten like a small, unknown niggle. Again he embraced her, and he too could feel the sense of loss, frustration, and the anger of *why?*

"Come on," she said at last. "We're no good to people like this, are we?" She reassured herself, blowing her nose again, escaping his hold. He looked at her with big doe eyes but didn't speak. He put his arm around her shoulder and pointed her in the direction of defaced shop.

> Charles:
> I couldn't help her. I could not stop the wailing, the cries, the language spilling from

her lips. I did not want to strike her, but the firemen became twitchy. I slapped her face. It was only to stop her from hysteria. I could do no more to contain her.

I am saddened by the strike. Her mind was lost, so uncontrollable.

She calms. Then we help the injured. We have to improvise with some of the surgical procedures. Stopping blood loss is an utmost concern. As is getting the patients out of the fragile buildings and into a safer environment. The raid continues overhead; incendiaries now drop onto some of the other houses a street away. Smoke billows in the airash strangles are breathe. The light is now fading. Cyril is making progress with shifting the bus. The bodies have been removed and stretcher bearers carry them to the back of trucks to be stored for their families to collect later. The hole in the ground will be a task to fix with limited resources and manpower, although the women have stepped in with keeping the roads clear and filling in the craters.

I remember poor Eunice's face when we pulled her friend from the rubble of the maze wing and her very kind words to accommodate us up by the heath. It's a ways up there, and we had best make good time. I know her grandmother would have hot food for us and warm, clean clothing and perhaps a bath. The thought of the bath and knowing of a god send of wholesome meal ahead of us keeps my mind focused through the madness around.

The firemen and I attend to a house where some elderly people have been trapped. I step carefully through the crumbled, burnt hallway to administer medicine to those inside. The firemen have pulled out several unidentifiable bodies. The bodies are black and charred, burnt so that the skin hangs still bubbling, revealing ligaments in the hands and arms like some poorly over-cooked roasted pig. Their lips are black from inhalation, and their faces are hollowed in the cheeks, disfiguring them. I step over one body and horror strikes my soul. The knarred, bony, charcoaled hand of an old lady grabs my ankle. I peer down into her sunken face; her eyes are whitened and blind from the heat; her mouth moves slowly and painfully; "Help me," her lips form. I know in my heart that I cannot save her, and I cruelly pry her hand from my leg and continue to advance forward to find someone I can. I then leave the house to seek out my companion.

Someone is calling from behind the row of houses. Some of us dash around to find a young woman pinned under a collapsed iron

# THE MIRROR

roof of an Anderson air raid shelter . She is in intense pain. A fireman, his nickname is Tiny, tries to support the part of the roof that has wedged the poor victim. He tries to use torn pieces of timber to stabilise a working platform. He tries to raise it from the crushed woman, using makeshift leavers, but she continues to scream, "Let me die." I administer a shot of morphine to ease her pain. I hear the echo of her legs scraping at the metal roofing, knowing too well it's the sound of gaping bones making the scratching noise each time she tries to kick out to free herself. Alas, the woman passes in a few minutes. I utter a short prayer in French and Latin for what it is worth, informing Tiny of the grim news.

We still need to remove her twisted, broken body. The only way to pull her warm dead body free is by tearing away the trapped lower limbs from the main body. The cooling blood oozes out. It cracks the bones of the femur, popping the patella, leaving the leg from the tibia trapped under the roof. Tiny assists by chopping at the legs with his axe. My head is covered in sweat and the stitches sting from the salt. A carrier comes to remove the remnant of the contorted, cooling body. No words are exchanged on the events or condition of the contorted body.

I take leave, thanking Tiny, and I mop my brow, continuing my search to assist others.

I call to Samantha, who has finished binding up a small child's leg in the doorway of a blown-out shop. She informs me the child has rickets and desperately needs vitamins and something called physiotherapy. There is not much we can offer at the hospital presently. I retrieve the apple from my bag that I took from Samantha's cooling cupboard and give it the boy. He is stunned but grateful. Samantha peers at me, glancing at the apple. I just grin a knowing grin. She laughs. The boy bites at it greedily, so no other can take a bite. His mother is calling for him from down the street. She is crying, and her voice is croaking. I nod at Sam, and we disappear before she finds us feeding the lad.

We look back at the bike. We decide now with darkness about us to use the tube to Hampstead.

Twenty-first century:

"I'm hungry," harps Jenny. "We should have eaten that pizza; we have been here ages."

Stephan rebukes her. "Christ, Jenny, do you not understand what we are dealing with here? I thought you guys were nuts... now I think I am!" He glances at Simon, who has not stopped reading. His mouth is aghast at some of the scenes he is reading.

"Poor Sammy, poor, poor Sammy." He then glares up at Rossini.

"Why is she there and not here? Hmmm?" His eyes are now narrowing. Stephan glares across at the medium.

"I do not know why you keep asking me such questions." She then points a gnarled finger at Simon. "I keep telling you, you have the answers. In here, in the stomach, not from the brain." She pokes his podgy tum.

"You know?" Stephan cross examines "Do you?"

Simon shakes his head. "It doesn't make sense."

Stephan now pages through the diary. "How much more is there?"

"Quite a bit." Simon fingers it.

"Well, Jenny and the Medium should go home. Why don't you come up to one of the dorms with the diary, Simon, and we can try and figure out what to do in comfort. If that's okay." He suggests. Jenny nods from tiredness. Rossini is delighted not to be held accountable. "If we get caught in here..." Stephan draws a throat-cutting line.

Simon stashes the diary under his coat. They turn off the lights and await the all-clear from Stephan to quietly lock up the library. Simon happily follows Stephan up to the male nurses' dorm.

Stephan finds a quiet, unoccupied room. He pulls a bottle of red wine from his bag, finds two mugs, and offers one to Simon. Simon puts the diary onto the small table and both men slurp the wine while they read.

Samantha:
The tube was not something desirable to travel on. It was hot, filled with billowing cigarette smoke and unwashed, weary, bleary-eyed travellers.

The platforms were packed with the bombed-out homeless. Children were entertaining themselves, women and older men were singing songs of victory and general togetherness. It was known as the British spirit of the blitz. It felt different to her now. She had been fighting through the past few days, and the small pain in her hand was now nothing to complain of. She was grateful for who she was and for the people that she had newly encountered. Eunice would be there at the house waiting for them. A dispatch runner had informed the unit before they left that there was a message for them from St Thomas.

Samantha stood in the clacking wooden carriage; it swayed back and forth and rattled deafeningly. Each station they passed through had its own set of refugees. Some of the stations she recognised because the tiled and checked walls were still the same today, she thought. Then her mind scrambled in a panic. Today was 1941, whatever day it was. What if she was stuck here? What if this was her destiny? Her thoughts were cut short as someone began to sing behind her. She giggled – someone singing on the tube! Wow, that's advancement.

# THE HOUSE ON THE COMMON

They reached the address up by the heath. It had a large Victorian frontage with its grand pillars and airy windows. A large gas lamp stood empty and unlit outside. Sam cocked her head and thought about *The Lion, The Witch and the Wardrobe, Mary Poppins, Peter Pan*. Eunice's grandmother was at the door beckoning them in out of the now lightly falling rain and the raid, the raid that seemed so far away from them. She was a stoutly, clean, aged woman. Her tiny form seemed to have had far better days. But her hair was neatly groomed, and her clothes were well pressed and starched. "Come in, come in." She waved to them. "Catch death of cold out in this!" Her accent was strong northern Irish, perhaps Belfast.

"Let's be having you," she remarked, taking the coat off Charles and shaking the rain off of it. "And you, miss." She looked up and down at Sam's attire, but didn't comment. "Let's have your little jacket then, miss." Again, shaking down the coat. "I'll hang these in the kitchen where they will dry quicker." She folded the items over her arm. "Go through and warm yourselves. I think Eunice and that young man need some sensible company, if you know what I mean... no, ah, hanky panky under my roof!" She grinned and winked, shooing them forward. "There's a nice drop of Irish malt if you want some, sir."

"Thank you, Mrs O'shea. Please, call me Charles. I am deeply grateful for your hospitality."

"Don't be daft. It's the least I can do. You've been so kind to all those girls and staff and, my goodness, what you have done to mend all those poor souls."

Samantha had already entered the front room to get warm and get a glug of whisky. She interrupted Eunice and the young medic, who both darted apart. Obvious to Sam, they had been playing tonsil tennis. The man's hands were now in his pockets, with a wee twinkle in his eye.

"Beg pardon." Sam clears her throat. "Don't mind me." She then winked at Eunice. Eunice gave an unsettling laugh. Sam pushed her lips together tightly in an expression of "I will keep me mouth shut".

"You didn't hang about," she teased the young medic. He shrugged his shoulders and gave a deeply happy smile.

"She's beautiful," he spoke, modestly low. "No point in waiting for someone else to snatch her up, is there?" he chortled. Eunice was now blushing. The young man cocked his head. "You and the doc?"

Now it was Sam turn; she shrugged her shoulders. "I'm not sure what goes on in that head of his. Real cool on the outside."

"What's cool?" a gentle voice echoed from the door.

"Miss here was saying the rain," the young man responded.

"I am Samantha. I never did catch your name." The young man grinned, pouring Charles a large glass of whisky.

"May I?" Sam put out her hand. The young man looked at Eunice for permission. Eunice nodded and accepted a drink herself.

Charles handed his glass to Sam and accepted the second large glass.

"George," the medic said, tipping his hand against his head, sweeping back his hair. "George Harry James Tomlinson, medic... er, erm, training to be, that is." He nodded towards the doctor.

Sam nearly spat out her whisky and started choking violently. Charles gave her a gentle pat on the back, cocking his head quizzically. "Bit strong, miss?" the young man jabbered on. "Want some water in it?" Sam shook her head.

"No, that'd be sacrilege." The fire crackled behind them. Her eyes were wide and fixed on the young man. No, she thought, no... impossible. She glugged hard at the amber fluid, making a rather rude slurping sound. They all chuckled at Sam's expense. "Beg pardon."

Dinner was called, and they all washed their hands in the kitchen before sitting around the large kitchen table. Its plates and cutlery were all neatly laid out. The coats were now hanging from a makeshift indoor washing line at the far end by the blacked-out windows. The room was lit with candles and wall sconces, and the Aga churned out the heat.

A big stew pot sat brimming in the middle of the table, and all the tummies began growling at the wonderful aroma. A loud bang made them pause briefly. Eunice's grandmother stood at the head and prayed. She prayed the Lord's Prayer and for the safety of her son, Eunice's father, who was out on the battlefront. She prayed for the resting of the souls and thanked the lord for their livelihood and food.

Sam sat down and asked what the stew was.

"Oh, rabbit, of course. We have an abundance up here. You know, being next to the heath. We seem to be able catch more than the bloody daft butcher. Well." Eunice laughed and grinned, knowing what was coming next. "Well, that crafty bloody cat is a godsend. He caught two yesterday, hence a great pot full. It's like it had known we would have guests!"

She let a roar of laughter and toasted: "Heres to mighty Niger and his sidekick, Sooty."

Sam did not care what it was she was devouring; she had never felt so hungry and thirsty.

"Have plenty of homemade lemonade whilst we can, and there is some tea on a pot on the stove."

"Thank you, Mrs Oshea, for sheltering us and well, mmm, the food." Sam beamed.

"You'll be welcome." Mrs Oshea nodded in polite gratitude to the whole table. George was too busy devouring the stew; with a mouthful, he nodded and tried to speak some words of gratitude, which made Sam giggle – her grandfather always spoke while eating, and her great-grandmother always told him off for it. Eunice reprimanded him by digging him in the ribs.

Silence fell as they all ate, and the cats sat smugly by the warming Aga.

Charles interrupted the clickty clack of cutlery being vigorously scraped across porcelain. "Mrs Oshea, I have to go to Parliament tomorrow to do the check-ups on... you know, erm... can Samantha be of assistance to you? Rather than have her at the hospital; it has been a terrible day." Charles smiled sweetly at Sam.

"You didn't attend that bus scene, did you?" Both Sam and Charles nodded their heads slowly in distaste of the previous scene .

"It was dreadful... really dreadful." Sam's words were weak and mumbling.

"Oh, my dear... and poor Rachel." Mrs Oshea eyes were brimming with comfort to Eunice.

Eunice bowed her head and spoke softly. "She did not suffer, Grandmother. I was there, and the priest was also. At least we had the priest, Father Michael."

Mrs Oshea bowed her head in respect. Silence fell for a few moments and nobody moved.

"Well," Mrs Oshea brightened suddenly, "there will be a big band dance at the coliseum tomorrow night." She smiled affectionately at them all. "As long as you take the young lady and have some fun, it will be all right." Charles smiled.

"Of course there's just one problem: clothing."

"Oh, it's all right. We have odds here and there. Don't worry, sir, she will be dressed as fine as she looks."

"Thank you, Mrs Oshea."

"Now, stop thanking me and make yourself useful." She ushered the men to fill a tin bath for the girls to soak in upstairs in front of the fire. The girls were instructed to wash up and then to relax in a warm bath. The men happily lugged the water up the stairs and retired to the whisky.

The rooms and beds were sparse but clean and tidy. A lot of pride had gone into pressing and cleaning the house.

Sam wondered what her journey would be tomorrow. But knew she was in a safe place with kind, safe folks.

The tin bath was set up in front of the roaring fire in one of the upstairs rooms and each person who entered the water had to be careful not burn their rear end on the hot metal siding the fire. The room brimmed with steam, soap, and the rich, earthy wood and coal crackling in the flames.

Eunice sat on the edge of a dressing table , swinging her legs and asking about Sam's bag and her odd clothing. She asked why Sam had a tattoo of a parrot in the middle of her back. Sam thought quickly and said it had been done for an experimental dare, but that she liked it. Eunice agreed it was indeed a beautiful creature, but was it ladylike? "sort of things blokes had , navies and that" But she thought no more of it. She realised Sam was well travelled and there were things Eunice did not understand or did not want to.

The girls chatted whilst the others bathed. Sam discovers that Eunice's mother died three years prior from pneumonia. It was a sad affair and her father was posted back to Poland soon afterwards. She remained in her grandmother's care, and her father swore he would return. Sam's heart lunged at the thought that Eunice could be left with just her gran. Sam knew the history of Poland and how it was raped of everything it had to offer by the Germans and then by the Red Army. She didn't speak of it or of the missing thousands of Polish guards, massacred by Stalin's henchmen who blamed the disappearances on the Nazis. The bodies were scattered in mass graves along the deep forests of Katyn near Smolensk. Only when the Nazis pushed through towards deep Russian soil were the bodies exhumed, and false documentation

# THE MIRROR

was created saying that the Nazis had slaughtered them all. Stalin was a cunning man, which wrenched Sam's heart. Churchill needed to be warned of the hidden scams, lies, and backbiting. How? How the hell? Was that why she was here? To help?

The men stumbled the stairs after the women's baths, and each took a soak until the water could not clean anyone anymore. They sang whilst they bathed, causing the whole house to fall into laughter. Their songs were not any less rude or silly.

The girls shared a room and the men were put in the top room of the house. The stairs were creaky: a cunning plan to stop any mischief going on under Mrs O'shea's roof.

However, the men had a plan.

In the early hours, when the house was still and the thunder of the bombings was still pounding the city, the men crept out of their room. Their heads were giddy with the malt and the smoking of Charles's pipe. They were relaxed and unafraid of Mrs Oshea's tyranny. They could hear the old girl snoring loudly; it echoed through the tall stairwell.

Sam was fitful, afraid to sleep in case she woke somewhere unfamiliar. Eunice was well away, dreaming of rabbits and fairies. A chink of small candle light entered through an increasing crack in the doorframe. A head appeared above in it with a shushing finger against its lips. It was George. He pointed at Eunice. Sam crept out of bed, revealing that she was actually wearing very little. George gaffed at the site. Sam shushed him. She gently rocked Eunice to wake up. Eunice's blurry eyes then fixated on the door. She leaned forward to have a clearer view, and then a big smile formed on her face. She giggled naughtily. George beckoned her. Eunice pulled the covers off and slid out, stretching. She whispered "What you be doing? You'll get your head bashed in by Granny."

"Ah, that'd be worth it; I would die a happy man." He grinned.

Eunice glanced at Sam, who shooed her on. Sam turned to get back into bed as the pair disappeared behind the door and up the creaky stairs. Another face appeared: Charles's. His face was dancing with mischief and it was obvious he was intoxicated but very happy.

"Hello," he whispered. "Can I come in? I'm homeless. Well, I've been shafted out." He was beaming and did a wink-wink, nudge-nudge. Sam nodded. He clumsily fastened the door and heard the snoring downstairs change to that piggy sound people make when they awake because their own snoring wakes them. Sam shushed him. He crept to the edge of the bed and plunked himself down, making it squeak. He was clad only in scraggy pyjama bottoms, untidily fastened with a spindly thread at the front. If he moved incorrectly, everything would fall out.

"What's up?" she enquired innocently.

"Him, upstairs." He grinned. "Horny toad can't seem to stop it from rising." He laughed and slapped his hand across his knee. Sam giggled; it was the first time she had seen him so relaxed. She remembered Jenny's vision of him in the mirror dancing naked. He did a little hiccup squeak, followed by a small belch and tiny fart, which he tried to disguise, but he giggled as it escapes.

"You're funny," she squeaked.

"Funny-weird or ha-ha funny?" he babbled.

"You. You're so hidden and now look at you."

## THE MIRROR

His face hurt for an instant, and then he smiled. "God, you're beautiful... oh, and that aroma!" He spun his head about. "It's driving me crazy, smelling you around my home all the time." He chuckled, leaning forward to Sam's bunched knees under the covers. They could hear movement around upstairs, and they both froze for a second as the noise increased. Charles chuckled.

"Probably having trouble with the springs," he slurred, swaying his head about. You all right? I didn't mean to hurt you earlier. It was horrible, wasn't it? Really horrid. You were quite right. Nazi bastards." He patted her knees.

Sam stared at him, bemused and a little frightened.

"Do you like me?" He cocked his head to one side, smiling sweetly, fluttering his eyelids. "I like you... a lot. Where did you learn to ride such a beast, that motorbike. Cor, wow. Mad, my head spun." He patted her knees again.

"I know." Sam smiled.

"Oops. I ,well, such a beautiful thing and the music, the wind, and, well, you," he explains, flaying his arms around. "I mean, what can a man do but to behold such wonderment?"

Sam could hear his words from his diary. His hidden self. A man on the edge, in need of want.

"Your voice is getting louder. You'll wake Granny, and then what will we do ?"

"I could give her a shot to keep her quiet," he jokes, pressing his finger against his nose.

"You wouldn't? ... Would you?"

He shook his head.

"There are some ethics still I have!" He giggles, patting her knees again. "I still believe you are beautiful."

"You're drunk," she whispered. "Do you know what you're saying?"

He nods. "I remember everything... most of the time." He chuckled. "I m sorry, miss, we got carried away, and I needed to get those people out of my head." His face falls into disappear of torcher at the reminder of the grim scene.

"Here, come sit next to me. You have next to nothing on, and it's a cold night." She pulls back the covers, revealing a very scantily clad Samantha.

"Cor blimey." He grinned. "You sure? A fool like me?"

"Get in," she barked. "You're freezing."

He stumbled in, needing assistance, and tugged at the tightly tucked in blankets. His breath was heavy with whisky and opium. He pulled the covers back over himself and lay on his side facing her. She lay down with him. "Just hold me," he whispered. "I can't do anything to harm you, Miss Samantha. It stopped working an hour ago, with the pipe. Hope you don't mind."

Sam held him close to her. She was glad to have his warm body for company, just as he was, all drunk and stupidly folly.

She embraced him, and soon his body relaxed, stopped shivering, and was deep in slumber. Sam, however, found it more difficult to sleep, being sober and with the creaking of the bed upstairs.

She awoke with Eunice shaking her. Sam peered around the room, bleary-eyed and unable to see properly. She must have removed her lenses without realising. She blinked up into Eunice's massive grin. "Well?" Eunice grinned.

"Well, what?" Sam barked, knowing she was in the bed alone.

"You know..." Eunice grinned. "What was it like?" She was grinning even more.

"What?" Sam was now agitated.

"George... was wonderful. So masculine. So damn randy!" she squealed.

"Oh, god, Eunice," Sam bleated, pulling the covers over her head.

"Ah, I can barely walk," Eunice continued. "I didn't know you could do it so many ways." She grinned and pulled the covers away from Sam's head.

"Well? You're going to tell me, lover girl." Eunice jabbed at Sam's ribs.

"Eunice!" Sam bellowed. "Bloody hell, girl." She tugged back at the covers.

"Oh, we are grumpy. Not much sleep, aye?" She winked at Sam.

Sam had enough. She threw back the bed clothes, leapt out, and shoved Eunice out of the way. She stumbled slightly, as she couldn't quite see her footings. Sam grabbed her bag from under the bottom end of the bed and exited the bedroom, slamming the door behind her.

She mumbled, "Nosey cow..." and growled in the back of her throat.

The house had an indoor toilet, but it was downstairs through the back end of the kitchen. She strode straight through the kitchen, not blinking or acknowledging anyone. The two men nearly choked on their tea. Mrs O'shea dropped her spoon and called after the scantily clad Sam.

Charles sprang to his feet in pursuit. Mrs O'shea pushed

him back into his seat, waving a finger at him. "Oh, no you don't."

She rapped on the door. She stood motionless, listening. Sam was sobbing.

"Come on, dear, it's all right. Come have some tea," she whispered through the door. "Gave us a fright like that. The men, well, they're still wiping tea from their chests." She rapped again. "What is the matter?"

Eunice appeared behind Mrs O'shea. "She all right?"

Eunice shrugged her shoulders. "She was really grumpy when I woke her. All snappy."

"Oh, all right." Mrs O'shea nodded. "Let's leave her alone."

"I need to go," Eunice harped.

"You just went ten minutes ago, girl.. You be all right?" she asked her.

Eunice, now reddening, said "It's all right; I can wait... too much tea." She wryly smiled.

She turned and George was grinning and winking at her.

She blushed some more as she caught Charles's eye.

Charles stood up and gently approached Mrs O'shea, who was still guarding the door.

"May I try?" he whispered.

She nodded.

He pressed his face hard against the door, willing himself through it.

"Samantha..." He gently tapped the door. "Samantha, please come out. You need something to eat," he begged. "You're still suffering from yesterday. It's okay," he assured, "the raid finished about six o'clock, before dawn. They won't be back for hours yet." He pressed his hand against the door. Slowly, the sobbing ceased, and Sam unbolted the door. He thrust the door open wide and grabbed her, embracing her firmly. Her body jerked and the tears flowed. She let out a big wail, burying her head in his chest. George, Eunice, and Mrs O'shea just stood silently aghast.

Charles spoke directly to Eunice pulling Sam from the doorway . "Get me a blanket, quickly." Then at Mrs O'shea, he said, "Tea, very sweet." Eunice was gone and back in a flash, clutching the blanket. "George, stoke up the fire."

"Be devil, what's happened?" Mrs O'shea questioned, concerned.

"Shock and cold," Charles snapped. "Come on, George, put your back in it." George was fiercely prodding and feeding the Aga.

Charles wrapped Sam in the blanket. He pulled up a chair and wedged her as close to the Aga as he could. He sat thinking a moment while Mrs O'shea made the tea. The other pair stood waiting for further instruction. Charles squatted next to Sam's still-sobbing body; his arm was around her waist, under the blanket. The opium pipe helped him relieve the shock and mental torment, but what else could he do? George struck up a cigarette and puffed heavily on it, offering it to anyone whom was in want of nicotine.

Mrs O'shea poured the tea, adding honey for sweetness. She shooed away the other pair for some privacy and closed the kitchen door, allowing the two to huddle alone.

Sam eventually took the cup from Charles's hand and sipped it slowly under his instruction. He ran his finger along the edge of her eyes, catching the tears.

"Here." He offered his clean handkerchief for her nose.

She blew it hard. Snorting, she made eye contact, murmured sorry, and snorted again.

He embraced her again, removing the cup from her hand as not to scold her. Stoking her hair from her face, he kissed her forehead. Then he held her again.

He sat back on his haunches and gazed at her. "I meant everything I said last night," he whispered. "I'm sorry if I was stupid." He coughed. "Forgive me."

She smiled now, thinking of how funny he was and of the gentleness that was oozing from every part of his being.

"You were dead funny," she giggled. He giggled too, and then their eyes met and locked. They held for a moment. He leaned forward and gently kissed her salty, tear-sodden lips. His hand slowly cupped her wet face. Sam clasped the back of his neck, pushing her mouth hard against his lips, forcing his mouth to open.

The moment was interrupted by a slightly embarrassed cough from Mrs Oshea. "You're supposed to be fixing the girl, not eating her!" Charles stood up, away from Sam, to confront the glare of the old lady. Her hands were clasped tightly at the front. Her visage was very disapproving. "Let's be having you," she demanded.

Charles spoke firmly. "She seems to be recovering now," he informed her, now twitching from one foot to the other.

"Oh, I can see that all right!" she boomed. Sam started to laugh. The old woman put the fear of god into everyone, and of all the incidences, they got caught in this one.

Sam looked up at Charles and reached out to his hand. "Thank you," she smiled. "Thank you for being there." He squeezed her hand back. He gazed down, his eyes doe-like.

"Don't forget," he said "the big band tonight at the

coliseum. I'll meet you at the Princess of Wales Inn, and we will walk up." He winked. "You're beautiful."

Mrs Oshea gave him a sharp tap on his shoulder. He scooted out the door, but before Mrs O'shea could shut behind him, he blew her a kiss and winked again.

"Oh, those men." She shook her head. "He is rather dashing, though." She smiled briefly at Sam. "But not under my roof!" She pointed her finger. Sam just giggled.

Simon:

Simon awoke to his mobile bleating. It wasn't his alarm; it was a call. He didn't recognise the number and ignored it. But it kept ringing.

Stephan barked at him to answer the bloody thing, which he did on the fifth attempt.

His face went pallid. "It's the police," he flapped, shoving Stephan to wake up.

"What!" Stephan panicked. "What do they want?" he barked.

Simon shushed him. When the call ended, Simon was panicking.

"It's Sammy. They found her!"

"What? Is she alright? Where?"

"He said something about the London Zoo. And really bizarrely, he said she had broken into the giraffe compound. They said she seemed to be under the influence of drugs and alcohol. No ID, just wearing some skimpy wartime costume dress. I don't know." They both looked at each other oddly.

"Come on, Mr Hunkster, we have a slut to catch." He laughed.

"Yeah," giggled Stephan as he found his underwear from somewhere across the far end of the small room. "Mind you, he is a bit of a dirty so-and-so, writing that all down in his diary." He pranced around, making his willy bob up and down to taunt Simon. "What do you reckon of my mighty stallion?" He grinned.

"We don't have time for that!" Simon bleated. "Well..." He grinned, standing up naked from the bed himself, showing his full erection.

Samantha:

Eunice and George left hand-in-hand, heading off to the hospital, leaving Sam in Mrs Oshea's care.

"Well, we need to get a few things from the ration book, and then we will be off to feed the girls at the factory at lunchtime," Mrs O'shea declared. "I run the kitchen!" she announced with a puffed chest. What a surprise, thought Sam. "I put your dirty clothes in the tub this morning, and they should be dry tomorrow with any luck. You look grand in Eunice's clothes. Why do you like the trousers so much? You have pretty legs; hope you'll show them off later," she teased.

First, they headed out with the basket and ration book. Mrs Oshea picked up dried eggs, milk, some beans, bread, a small block of butter and a packet of hard biscuits and bartered for some fresh vegetables. There was no sugar or tea.

They placed the goods away in the pantry back at the house, and then they set off to catch the bus. Sam had no money, so Mrs O'shea paid for two 2d tickets.

Sam felt very uneasy mounting the bus after what

had happened the day before. But there was no raid, and everyone was busy confidently continuing on with their day to day work.

It was a long journey; the bus had to change its route several times. At one point, panic set in as the road was suddenly closed due to an unexploded device. They got onto trams as they drew nearer into the city.

# THE BREWERY

Mrs O'shea didn't stop talking the whole way: to other passengers, to Samantha, tutting and moaning about the state of affairs, no tea, men and their randy spirits and the lack of them. Sam kept her eyes fixed out of the window as the tram trudged its way slowly along. Christ, she thought, I am going to have to get out and push. She sat with her chin on her hand like a bored child, but she found herself lost in Charles's kiss. Stupid, she kept thinking... stupid Sam... it all ends in hurt... stop it, Sam. She kept thinking about him over and over again until she started laughing at her moronic thought pattern. God, she never felt like this with Johnnie.

They reached the factory and Sam had to be woken from her thoughts and dragged from the tram. She had no idea where she was. Sam was blurry eyed, and her eyes felt sore from the constant wearing of her contact lenses. She panned the area. It was somehow familiar. They had crossed the Thames at some point, and she was now in view of St Paul's. She scratched her head and tried to place the buildings. It came to her like a bolt. She was on the South

Bank. She nearly toppled over from the vast differences and some familiarities. The Victorian embankment was still adorned with its twisted iron lamps, busy with moored tugs. Men and women were cleaning, fixing, and welding the boats. She viewed the bombed wharfs, the mashed rubble still smouldering miserably. All about were docks, cranes lifting cargo to and from boats, the sound of the clanking of chains, and the calling and shouting of directions from boat to crane to dock. The was the smell of oil, steam, and stale, stagnant water.

"Come on, let's be having you," the droning voice rang in Sam's ears. She had learnt to switch it off on the bus journey, even when they had changed buses and had to walk a small few yards for a different stop.

"Come on, girl, we've a force to feed." She elbowed Sam into action. Sam was still trying to decide where the hell she was. Then she looked up at the building's doorway... the Lion Brewery!

Crap, it gets blown to bits, she recalls, and she hesitantly steps down inside.

The waft of the hops was intoxicating; it made her mouth drool. How she wanted a cool glass of beer. How she wanted to be away from the hell around her but not without Charles. It was mostly women there, under the guidance of a few older gentry, working and turning the hops in huge bubbling vats. Others at the opposite end of the factory were bottling, barrelling, packaging, and rolling the crates for transport. Some were using heavy machinery and controlling the dock cranes. Sam was quickly ushered through the distillery to the kitchen. Some of the women wolf-whistled at Mrs O'shea, knowing they were in for some good grub.

The kitchen was austere. There were huge metal tubs that were almost as big as the vats, or so Sam thought. Mrs O'shea' s voice reverberated around the room. "Right, let's stoke up the stoves and get some hearty food for these younglings."

Huge wood-burning stoves soon filled the air with an intense, sticky heat. Mrs O'shea started to peel potatoes and beckoned Sam to do soothe same. The knives were blunt, and Sam's hands hurt. The scar was sore from the fluid of the potatoes, and Mrs O'shea made her chop cabbage and carrots and fill the pans with water for boiling the broth. There was no salt or pepper to add; the broth was quite bland. It would subside hunger, but still it was bland.

The workers came when the horns blasted, each section forming an orderly queue and manners were restored, apart from the odd joke about the old men on site being surrounded by women.

Sam sat and joined a group that had snuck a keg of beer to the table. They all looked up innocently but with a hint of guilt in their eyes.

"Don't mind me," Sam started. "I wouldn't mind some, though, if there's enough to spare," she asked very politely.

One of the women addressed Sam. "What kind of an accent is that," her voice boomed in broad cockney, scowling.

"It's South African," Sam politely replied.

"African?" the woman laughed, almost losing her head scarf. "You be the wrong colour for an African, kind of a bit white to me."

# THE MIRROR

Sam flinched but continued addressing the woman's ignorance.

"It's a Dutch/French colony on the peninsula of Africa, right at the bottom. Trading ports, sugar cane, oil, fruit, linens, spices."

The woman cocked her head. "What you doing here, then? And why is it you don't sound French-like?"

"It's a blended language; it's multicultural."

"So," another piped in, "can you speak black?"

Sam rolled her eyes. "So can I have a mug of beer, please?"

"Yeah, why not," the second one nodded. "Though. don't tell Irish we got it." She did the finger throat-cut signal. Sam laughed.

"*Ja sy is'n stryd byl!*" Sam laughed. They all laughed nervously. Sam took one mighty glug from the jar. "*Probeer jy woon saam met haar.*"

A voice sung from the other end, its sound much more fluid and deeper than the other girls, "*Nie sy lyk soos 'n wesp toe sy slaap ook?*"

Sam just about fell laughing. The first women laughed too.

"She does speak black!"

A tall black woman stood up from the other end and pulled her chair up and sat next to Sam. Sam explained the joke. "Yes," she said through tears of laughter, "she does. She looks like she has swallowed a wasp most of the time. That's probably why she keeps her mouth buzzing."

The girls all fell about laughing. "Do you want some jokes?" Sam barked. "Sex is like snow," Sam continued, "you never know how many inches you are going to get or how long it will last."

The whole place fell into disarray. The black woman spoke: "What did the elephant say to the naked man? How do you breathe through something so small?"

They all rolled around, glugging the ale.

"Okay... okay, okay," flapped Sam, "how do you know when a cat's done cleaning himself? He's smoking a cigarette."

The first woman piped up through her tears. "What's worse than being raped by Jack the Ripper? Being fingered by Captain Hook!"

The women's laughter could be heard across the distillery.

Another woman chipped in: "How does a Welshman count his sheep? One, two, three, hello darling, five, six..."

One more butted in: "A farmer is lying in bed with his wife and grabs her boobs and says, 'If you could get milk out of these, we could sell the cow.' He then grabs her vagina and says, 'If we could get eggs from this, we could sell the chickens.' At that point, she grabs his dick and says, 'If you could get this up, we could get rid of your brother!'"

They all laughed, making their bellies hurt. It was the first time Sam had laughed in days. She turned and spoke in Afrikaans to the black lady, "*Lirieke he natte ikzelf!*" And the black woman laughed with her.

The first women asked what was said, so the black woman translated: "She wet herself laughing so hard!"

That was it. Sam's jug got filled again. She was taking another enormous gulp when somebody called out from near the kitchen door.

# THE MIRROR

"Christ, it's wasp-face coming!" The keg soon vanished under the table, kicked between the women's legs. Sam swallowed hard to get as much from the beer as she could. The other girls cheered as she downed it before Mrs O'shea came into view. Sam belched; they all laughed again.

Mrs O'shea was not amused and had a face of stone.

From behind Mrs O'shea, a grim–looking, smartly uniformed young telegram officer hesitatingly stepped forward. He could not have older than fifteen years old, with the light covering of facial hair, not worthy of being shaved. The women fell silent. Their faces were pallid, and their eyes were searching each others' faces. Sam sat silent, and a horrid feeling rose from her stomach. She didn't know what was coming, what was going to happen, but the women knew; they knew something.

The young man stepped forward towards the table. His eyes were terrified and search each of the women's faces. His hands trembled; the telegram shook. Mrs O'shea gave the boy an encouraging shove to get on with it.

Each woman scanned the boy's eyes; his eyes met them one by one until they stopped. He gingerly stepped forward, bowed his head, and spoke softly as he handed the telegram to the fourth woman to Sam's left.

"Sorry, miss." He stepped back, releasing the telegram.

The woman yelled out in intense pain, "*No... No... No!*" The boy scampered off with a tear in his eye.

The woman was inconsolable. She didn't open the telegram. The woman next to her did it for her, as the other women threw themselves around her to comfort her.

The telegram was read out: "Wing Commander Henry

John James Watson. Shot down during manoeuvres over France. No contact. Assumed missing in action."

That was all Sam could hear over the wailing of the woman who had just lost her husband.

Mrs O'shea pulled Sam to her feet and reprimanded her for having alcohol on her breath. Sam didn't care; her heart was torn out for the woman's loss.

She picked up the plates and took them to the kitchen, leaving the women to their sorrow. Sam felt goose bumps go up and down her spin every time she heard the woman wail in hysteria.

Mrs O'shea had her washing up, which stung the scar on her hand.

# THE BIG BAND

The journey back was more sobering. They took the underground as the raid started again. They dodged down the platform and had to evacuate the tunnel at one point because one station had received a direct hit, slamming down the whole system. Sam couldn't believe how everyone just kept about doing things. She hated the tube at the best of times, but it was filled with stagnant air and stale cigarette smoke and papers.

They returned back to the house in good time Eunice was already preparing the meal.

She smiled with an air of confidence and winked at Sam. "What will you be wearing for the big night, then?"

Sam shrugged her shoulders. "Don't have a lot left."

"My dresses seem to fit you. Why don't you have one of mine?" She smiled, twirling around happily. "Don't get it too dirty though, will you?" she teased. "Oh, Grandmother, we had a telegram," she called through the kitchen to Mrs O'shea, who was using the toilet.

Sam froze. Eunice winked. "It's from Daddy."

The toilet flushed and a partly dressed Mrs O'shea bolted

through the door, still hitching up her knickerbockers. Sam smirked.

A look was thrown.

"Well, child," Mrs O'shea demanded impatiently.

"He is fine, Grandmother; he sends his love and is missing your home cooking."

Everyone relaxed. Eunice produced the folded note and pressed it into Mrs O'shea hand, with soapy fingers.

Mrs O'shea, delighted at the good news, smiled for the first time; a small tear rolled down the edge of her face. "Good news..." she kept repeating in a whisper.

"Sit down, Grandmother. This won't take long." She shooed her out of the kitchen.

Eunice explained that she was cooking tonight because Granny does the brewery on Thursdays, and since they were out, they needed something quick and easy. So it was beans with potatoes and bread.

The three ate almost in silence but in a happy way. The cats sat again in the pole position, upfront by the Aga. No rabbits today, however, just mice.

Eunice was ushered out of the kitchen to get herself and Sam ready, being told that George would be there soon to escort them.

Charles:

He went back to his apartment to find that the damage was not as extensive as he first assumed. His evening suit had survived the bombing of the past two nights. He brushed off the dust and grime, picking at it. He folded it neatly in a large bag to take with him so he didn't waste time going back and forth. Odd, for a moment he saw faces in the mirror.

Faces crying, weeping. Faces he didn't recognise and hadn't seen before. He felt a cold shudder shoot down his spine and suddenly he was back in Sam's room.

"What now!" he thought, clutching his bag. He turned to the room, and his eyes were met by a roomful of people. Sam was one. Her hair was tatty, strewn, bedraggled; her eyes were red from weeping. She saw him, called out his name, and leapt to her feet. A young man stood next to the poof, clutching the poofs hand. His mouth was wide open in astonishment at Charles's appearance. A tall, foreboding man stood by the fireplace holding Sam's battered bag and Charles's diary.

"Oh my god!" Stephan cried out, "Oh my god," he cried again. The tall man didn't move.

Sam was there, clutching onto to Charles. "Thank god!" she exclaimed and kissed his cheek. "I didn't think I would see you again. I love you so." She kissed his mouth, pulling him into her strong embrace. The man in the corner enquired who he was. Before he could reply or even attempt to understand, he was back looking through the glass.

His mind, racing from the overwhelming response from Samantha, had trouble concentrating on his health checks with the MPs. She had smelt of pipe smoke, alcohol, and sex. The way she kissed him, the aroma, her lips, and her body lustfully curving into him.

He led himself down into the secluded doctor's private chamber for the assessment within the walls of the House of Commons. He found some of the lords and Parliamentary members somewhat arrogant. Some were in denial of his given advice. Gout, impetigo, ecthyma ulcers, the usual suspects. Some were not keeping the open sores on their lower legs and feet clean and well dressed, creating oozing pustules. He despaired at the lack of hygiene expressed by some, their minds only focused on the next sip of alcohol into their distended livers.

In the gentlemen's club's room, the walls were clad in dark wood, and the room was furnished with high-backed leather chairs and a small bar with a rather nervous attendant. Here, the gathering of great minds would sortie. The air would be filled with raucous debate, swirling tobacco smoke, and the hefty aromas of alcohol.

He spent his lunch pondering the plight of Britain and the debate on America's new Magna Carta and whether they would step in and loan the British the support of their navy. Lord Halifax was certain they would comply, but Roosevelt was too afraid to drag in the USA into the war. Their economy just recovered from the financial depression of the twenties. Attlee sat puffing, debating with Ernie Bevan about Joseph Kennedy's opposing the involvement of the U.S. Navy. Charles discussed the increase of dysentery and questioned what could be done to clean the water supplies quicker and more efficiently. He suggested also that a campaign should be made for awareness of syphilis, hepatitis, and the general well being and that would support the avoidance of one-night stands that could cause an epidemic.

Churchill later joined them, chugging his cigar. Charles wafted the smoke away from his face, offering the gent his seat. Churchill barked at him that the physician appointed by the King should have the respect of the other gentry and shooed out Nye Bevan from his seat. Charles was embarrassed by the gesture, but they did as they were told by the intimidating presence of Churchill.

# THE MIRROR

After they finished the gentlemen's debate and some were slightly headier, he returned to his duty as private clinician.

A rouge, dirty old lord had to be checked for syphilis. "There is always one," thought Charles. Charles informed the gent that if he continued his philandering and fornication activities and continued spreading the disease, he would put the lord into isolation and publicly denounce him. He hated having to check the penis and anus, treating the scabs and sores as best as he could to ease comfort. He prescribed Salvasan. "He shouldn't be sticking it where he had," he thought in disgust.

Another chap needed to build up a shoe heel because his shorter leg was creating pain in his hip from hobbling. He suggested taking the shoe to a specialised cobbler up on Fleet Street.

He was glad his day over. He felt unclean and grimy; at least at the hospital he was scrubbed up and in a clean, sterile environment, not prodding around fixing someone else's misdemeanours and promiscuities.

He bathed in the private suite and steamed himself in the Turkish bath. He saw his friend Jack and paid him for more pipe tobacco. Jack smiled, handing over the packets, knowing it was good supply. Charles thanked the man and finished his grooming with a good, clean Turkish shave. He splashed up with his Old Spice and neatly combed and waxed his hair. His suit had been pressed, and he was pleased with the way he was attired, smiling within. Before he left the main building, the porter handed him another package, his pay for the day. Yes, he was ready to paint the town red and treat his new-made friends and some of his old friends.

They were all going to meet up the hill in Villiers Street. The inn was still standing amongst the ghastly, scarred fragments of the London streets.

He was late, but only just. He was puffed-out and pink-faced as he crossed the threshold. He had changed and bathed in the commons, allowed because he was a King's physician. His hair was neatly groomed, and his face was immaculately shaved.

Sam squealed when she saw him trudge through the doorway. He was indeed handsome. George felt a pang of jealousy at how well turned out the doctor was. But his mind soon returned to his beer and Eunice as she pinched his rear.

Sam threw her arms around Charles and kissed his cheek. She rubbed across his forehead; his stitches were almost unnoticeable. Charles, for a moment, froze in her embrace. The dress – it was the same one he had seen through the mirror earlier. "You all right?" Sam whispered, stopping his stunned look. "You look fab." Charles cocked his head and grinned.

"You scrub up well too."

"Cheeky," Eunice boomed, "spent an age getting her bleeding hair done!"

"You look beautiful... as ever." Eunice was making teasing gagging sounds.

"Come, doc. What are you having?" George beckoned him in.

"Lion Ale, please."

Sam shuddered momentarily.

"How did you get on with Mrs O'shea's?"

"Good, she paid me before we came out. I don't know what it means." She showed Charles the four coins: a shilling, a sixpence, and two pennies.

"That's okay for a few drinks tonight. You did well with that." He winked. "I'll buy, George," he called to the bar.

They sat supping on real ale for the good part of an hour. They headed up Villiers Street towards Trafalgar Square. It was odd for Sam seeing the old buildings, the bombed out gapping holes where all the new modern sites would be squeezed in. Charing Cross station was all rattled up with soot and dust.

The coliseum had not changed one jot; it was opened for one night only with the Joe Loss Orchetsra. It had been shut for some months due to safety reasons with the daily raids over London. Well, from the outside, thought Sam, it looked the same. It was different inside. The hall inside was crammed. People had jostled their way through the turnstiles, paying about 6d as they went in. It really was a big band night. The room was filled with swirling smoke and the sounds of joy; the outside guns and raid couldn't be heard amidst the frolicking.

Some home brews had been smuggled in and the four of them enjoyed taking part in the consumption of such concoctions. Poor Eunice nearly had her head blown off from the strength, but she was only a young girl, still only of late teens or early twenties,. Sam teased her, being the hardened drinker she was. George had to take Eunice to an open door to get her head clear. Sam learnt to follow Charles's foot steps and enjoyed flirting with him intensely. They danced in the stalls, and a part of the floor had been cleared in front of the stage for the more brave couples to show of their dancing talents. Small amounts of food were available, mainly what had been home cooked for an exchange of a couple of farthings and pence. Beers and gin were available from the bar, a little more pricy than the Princess of Wales, between 6d and 9d.

The evening came to an early end due to the raid intensifying outside, and the promoters were concerned for the safety of the spectators. Nobody minded, and everyone left in good order to the shelters or underground stations. George and Eunice made their own disappearance; George gave Charles a wink and a nudge as they stepped out into the rumbling night air.

Charles took Sam by the arm and escorted her in a gentlemanly manner to a cabbie and requested to head to Hampstead. The cabbie, surprised at the distance, requested the fare up front. Charles obliged, giving a substantial tip. It was probably the best fare the cabbie had had in weeks, and he grinned, chatting friendly all the way back to Hampstead.

"Was that expensive?" Sam asked. Charles grinned and nodded.

"Can't have you getting all sweated up on the underground." He beamed. "I did notice how uncomfortable you were." He slipped his hand around her waist and pulled her close into him. The cabbie looked over his shoulder, remarking how lovely the lady looked and what a lucky fella Charles was.

They sat cuddled up in a comforting silence, eyes on each other, their heads giddy from alcohol, unaware of the flashing, thundering sky.

George headed back with Eunice via the underground, only to be trapped at one station as the line closed. They spent part of their romantic night amidst other patrons trapped in the tunnels. But at least they had each other.

# THE COMMON

Charles and Sam reached the house, and the cabbie bid them farewell. Charles offered her the steps. She shook her head. "Can we walk? It's a fair evening." She pointed to the heath. "I know a good pathway along there." He obliged, taking her hand. "You know Churchill?"

Charles stopped in his stride and whispered, "Why are you asking?"

"There are some things you must know. When he goes to Carthage in Tunisia, he must take lord Mansion with him; he will be very ill. Fleming's antibiotics won't cure him. It will be sulphates," she continued, keeping up with Charles's nervously quickening pace. He listened, scanning the area for eavesdroppers. "Also, he is not to trust Eisenhower completely, or that crazy Russian, Stalin." Charles stopped and put his hand gently over her mouth to stop her speaking.

"Careful, Samantha. What you are doing, spilling gossip?"

"No, it's all true." She tried to explain D-Day and the Nazis forcing the Red Army back, the involvement of the USA and Pearl Harbor in the oncoming December. The cunning

## THE MIRROR

of Stalin, and the pressure on Churchill to advance in taking back France. The doodlebugs. Burma and the Japanese. The dog fights over the Pacific. The atomic bomb.

Charles listened intensely, watching and twitching for any passers by that could listen in. He teased her by saying that she was a gypsy fortune teller. But the details were so accurate, it disturbed him.

At last, Charles stopped and spread out his coat on soft heath, taking his pipe out. "Is that what you bought me here for?" he said, patting his coat for her to sit next to him. "To talk me to death? Come, relax. Let's watch the stars and see how many planes our gunners can blast into pieces." There was a glint in his eye.

He lit his pipe and puffed on it. He offered it to her. She tried it coughing on the first inhalation. It made her head giddy and her body feel tingly, and suddenly she was staring at the stars, bleating how wonderful there were. Her body relaxed, all the tension and torment of the day, the drama at forest gate and the stench of the broken sewers disappeared. She was filled with a strange sense of overwhelming euphoria. Her face grinning intensely.

Charles leaned up so she could see his face. He was Clark Kent in porn, she thought, grabbing at his neck, pulling him down onto her lips. She forced his mouth open with her tongue, devouring him; he obliged. Charles's hands wandered rampantly, searching out breasts and clumsily unclipping her bra. His lips fell over her neck as his hands caressed her breasts. Her hands pulled up the back of his shirt, allowing her to feel the skin of his back. Her body tingled with immense excitement and sexual hunger. She squeezed his buttocks.

He tore at her dress top, exposing her breasts to the night sky, placing his lips over her nipples, sucking at them, working them with his tongue. Both were groaning, breathing heavily with anticipation and lust. His hands moved down and up under her dress, finding her thighs and buttocks. She pulled at his braces and tugged at his belt, slipping her hands down his trousers front.

There she felt his full, hardened, huge erection; she worked her hands around it.

He spoke gently in small whispers of French lust.

He pulled at her knickers, flaying the small, delicate briefs to the heath.up on his knees, he pulled up her dress and pushed her knees apart. He found her clitoris with his tongue. She moaned, pawing at his head and whispered, "Please, I want to feel you. All of you."

He pushed his trouser further past his knees, mounted on top of her, fumbling with his fingers first, and entered her. She gasped out, pained by the sheer size of his penis, but she held tightly onto his buttocks. He was gentle; their bodies entwined, their mouths together, biting at each other's neck. She groaned, and he let out a huge cry, gasping for breath as he flooded her with a few hard thrusts. She groaned in ecstasy. He kept thrusting till he was empty.

He held her tight in his embrace. They stayed locked, happy. She felt him small now, but he didn't withdraw. He kissed her mouth tenderly, then hungrily with passion and lust. She felt him growing again inside her. This time it was more vocal, more harder thrusts, turning her over onto all fours. She then threw him to the ground and gyrated on top of him, almost paining herself by twisting back to feel him deep within her. The position pained her, but the pleasure, the high, kept her wanting more.

Again they moaned and whispered how much they enjoyed the other's body, lustfully wanting more.

The guns rang out overhead and the planes still ground their terrifying engines, scattering death and destruction.

The entwined, gyrating bodies were unaware of the night sky. They only knew of each other.

He lay down on top of her again, filling her again. Their heads were giddy from their sex; their bodies were all sweaty; their clothing was ripped impatiently.

This time, he pulled out. His moist penis glinted against the sky. He rearranged her dress to a dignified state. Turning on his knees, he reached over for her knickers. She could see how well toned his buttocks were now. She felt joyous and full of him. She had never experienced such multiple orgasms. She wanted more. She refused to put the delicate lace underwear on, and he grinned. He sat back on his haunches and adjusted his tangled braces and belt. "Here," he said, "have a breather." He lit up the pipe again, and they puffed giddily.

This time, she enticed him by lifting her skirt and then rubbing her hand against his penis. They performed once more.

# THE ZOO

She lay back on his coat, looking at the sky and the droning of the planes circling and thrusting their death upon their victims. He lay next to her, stroking and twirling her hair. He kissed her cheek and spoke softly. "We had better get you back. You know Mrs O'shea saw the cab pull up." He smiled cheekily. "She'll have my ear for having you out here." He laughed mockingly. He pulled her dress straight, buttoning up her front. "Oh dear, I think I may have torn it in haste." he admits.

He pulled himself to his feet and searched the grass for her underwear. When he turned back to face her, the coat and the sleepy sexually devoured Sam had vanished. He was left standing alone, his shirt tails flapping in the breeze and her knickers in his hand. He screamed, doubled over in despair.

She opened her eyes, gazing skyward, searching for his face. The sky was deep blue. Clean, fluffy white clouds danced in the high winds, but the smell! She was still lying on Charles's coat. Her dress was bedraggled about her, and

## THE MIRROR

her stomach was aching and sore. Her head spun as she tried to force herself to her knees. She called out for him, but there was no reply. She lay flat down again, staring up at the spinning sky. A long narrow triangular shaped face appeared in her vision, its eyes soft deep brown with long curled eyelashes. Startled, she let out a squeal , then tried to find her wobbly legs. The face came closer, and then the long grey sticky tongue licked the air around her. She was confused, scared, frozen with fear , couldn't move. Another appeared; it too was intrigued by the new arrival.

A voice rumbled some few yards away. "Oi! What do you think you are doing in there?" It was angry , defensive.

She lay still, cemented in fear, and her head was giddy, the world spinning from the pipe smoke. Oh, how she had enjoyed Charles. She smiled. Where was he? She thought she heard the clanging of gates and the hooves of horses. But the gait for the hooves was randomly odd too wide and much slower.

A burly faced man appeared, towering over her. He had a long pole in one hand, keys in the other. He was attired in overalls , with a crest insignia on the left breast. He murmured something she couldn't apprehend. She heard another man arrive, they stood pondering , peering down at her. "How the bleeding hell did you get in here?" the first man boomed.

She giggled in a murmur. "Where's Charles?"

"Who? You mean there's two of ya?" the second man commanded.

"Don't shout!" she whimpered, holding her hands to her ears.

A woman spoke, she appeared from behind the two

overalled men, crouching down by her. "You alright, miss? You been hurt?" Her words were kind and gentle. The woman was in neatly pressed blue trousers and a clean crisp white blouse . Sam shook her head.

"Where is Charles? He was here, just now." Panic reflected in her voice.

"I think we better call an ambulance and the police," the woman addressed the two men. "I think she's been drugged and dumped here... and by the looks of her, well..." The two men agreed, nodding thoughtfully."

"Can you stand, miss?" The woman offered a gentle hand to Sam. Sam nodded wearily but wobbled as she stood.

Steadying her, the woman wrapped the coat around her.

"This is his... he's such a wonderful man," Sam slurred.

"Mmm, not so sure about that. " Sam frowned back at the woman's comment. "Dumping you in here."

Sam looked around and gave a ghastly cry of despair. "*Charles!*" and burst into tears.

The giraffes, startled at the screech, herded towards the main gate the three wardens had come through.

As she sobbed, she felt his semen begin to trickle away from her, creeping down her thigh. She pulled the skirt of her dress tight around her legs, pulling the coat close for comfort and dignity.

"I really need to use the loo, please. Really, now," Sam demanded before she could be even more embarrassed. The woman agreed, but it was some few hundred yards' walk. Sam sniffed, sucking in the tears as they plodded towards the wardens block. She was back in the twenty-first century, surrounded by African giraffes, still wired up from

# THE MIRROR

the alcohol and pipe smoke. She ambled along in the gentle reassuring embrace of the female warden, throat coughing every few steps.

"You feel sick, miss?" the warden enquired soflty. Sam nodded.

"Christ, what the hell was in that smoke?" The familiar sound of sirens echoed in the distance, coming for her.

The warden waited outside the toilet door , allowing some privacy. Sam sat down on the toilet seat, releasing her bladder and bowel. The stomach cramps were awful, and the diarrhoea kept coming, making horrible spatterings. Then with a full twist of stomach cramp , the bile arose, she puked all over the floor. It splattering on her shoes and smattered in her hair. For a moment, the cubicle spun, and she bashed her head against the walls. The female warden frantically was rattling the door to open it. Sam wearily raised her her vomit coated hand and unbolted it.

"Jesus H. Christ!" the warden yelled and called urgently over her radio for immediate assistance.

The ambulance arrived in good time , with a police escort and the paramedics were soon in control.

"I'm a nurse," Sam kept murmuring. "I just got... don't know... my head and stomach." She started coughing.

The medic brought in oxygen and kept repeating questions. "Who are you? Where do you live? What did you eat? What did you drink? Are you allergic to anything?"

Sam murmured Simon's phone number and then passed out.

She came too in the back of the ambulance. A blanket was neatly wrapped around her. There was a saline line in one arm and oxygen mask.

The medic was addressing a young female police officer and the warden. The WPC noticed Sam's consciousness and stepped up into the ambulance.

"You all right, miss? Feeling a little better?" She smiled. "You okay if I ask you a few questions?" Sam looked over to get the medic's approval. She nodded.

"How did you get in the compound?" she asked.

Sam shrugged her shoulders. "I opened me eyes, and there I was... Africa." She grinned.

"You South African, miss?" Sam nodded. "What you been taking? Or," the WPC sniffed, "smoking?"

Sam shrugged. " We were being bombed; it was horrible, all those people with their heads missing and their torsos all charred and mangled. The smell... the smell was awful – cooked human flesh." Sam started coughing again behind the oxygen mask. The medic intervened.

"Big, deep breaths. Come on, that's it." The medic rubbed Sam's shoulders.

The WPC radioed, "I think we may need a liaison officer." Then she addressed the medic. "What do think she's had?"

"Bloods will show. We can't really give her anything in case it worsens the condition."

"What do you think? Amphetamines? Coke ? LSD? She's pretty delirious."

"Couldn't say, either, but yes, she kept murmuring about Nazi bastards."

The officer addressed Sam, whose eyes were rolling round her head. "What happened, miss? Were you attacked? You're safe now."

Sam couldn't reply. What would they believe? She sat silent, supping the oxygen, and slowly her head began clearing.

"You gave the warden a number. Who is that?"

Sam kept her eyes focused on the open door to stop the horizon from spinning. "My good friend, like my brother. Simon Wallis. He is a triage nurse like me and works between Guys and Waterloo."

The police officer nodded. "Should be here in a minute. Do you want us to tell him anything? You being dumped in the zoo? And, well, I hate to tell you miss, but the medics say you appear to have been sexually assaulted."

"Appear?" Sam questioned.

"We couldn't find evidence of another person. We checked the closed-circuit television. You seemed to just appear."

"Appear? What do you mean sexually assaulted?"

The medic stood grim-faced. "There are large traces of semen on your clothing, you have bite marks on various parts of your body, human bite marks, and I had to administer a pain killer because your abdominal and vulva are severely bruised. I am sorry to inform you." The medic peered up into the officer's eyes and continued. "It wasn't protected, either. I'm sorry."

Sam's eyes started welling up. He had refused her, but she had insisted and enticed him on, and now she was sore and unable to explain a possible non-rape.

She was relieved to hear a familiar voice: "Cor, the cavalry is here!" The WPC sprang to her feet and firmly shut the ambulance door.

Simon and Stephan were approached by the liaison officer as well as the WPC. Their faces were grim.

"Are you Mr Simon Wallis? Friend of Samantha Tomlinson?"

Simon paled; Stephan clasped Simon's hand. The officers noted the gesture.

"You are, sir?" the officers requested from Stephan.

"Her cousin. We grew up together."

"You South African?" the WPC chipped in. Stephan nodded. "Next of kin?"

Stephan nodded, and his gaze dropped. His eyes were now brimming.

"It's okay," the officer assured. "She is well, but there are some questions we need to ask."

Simon piped up. "Why is she in the back of an ambulance, then?"

"We think she may have been attacked. Does she take any medicines? Recreational drugs? Alcohol?"

"*Drugs?!* Hell no!" Simon stormed. "She loves her white wine, the lush." He continued, realising Stephan's hand and began flapping. "Why? What's happened to Sammy?"

"What was she doing last night? When did you last see her?"

Simon shuffled about nervously; his eye twitched from one officer to the other. Silence fell between them.

Stephan coughed. "You'll probably think we are mad."

The officers turned their head to Stephan's welling gaze.

Simon continued. He was still clutching the leather-bound book, his hands now tucked tightly around it, hugging it firmly. "There was a séance." The WPC groaned. "Well, there is this ghost in her flat. I think it's a ghost. And it came and took her," he bleated self-consciously.

"It took her?"

Simon nodded.

"Were you there?"

"No, Metal Mickey was, and that old walking fashion disaster was, but I didn't see her... it was dark."

"*Stop!* Are you guys experimenting with some new drug from the hospital stores?"

Simon flounced his hands on his hips. "I beg your pardon!" he hissed.

"Can we see her, please," Stephan interjected.

"You guys know of anyone that would harm Miss Tomlinson?"

Stephan looked at the book and then caught Simon's gaze. "No, but he may be a bit rough."

"Rough?" the officer squealed. "She was nearly turned inside out!"

"Told you he was big," Simon whispered into Stephan's ear.

"Pardon, sir?" the officer asked at Simon's whispering.

"Oh, just bragging." The officer wasn't impressed.

"What you got there, then?" the WPC requested.

"It's a diary... Sam's been reading it."

"Whose?" the WPC enquired.

"A World War II surgeon," Simon replied.

"May I?" the WPC asked.

"Don't lose it." Simon handed it over. The WPC starts thumbing through, flicking pages over and freezes on a page with her face aghast.

She looks up at Simon in bewilderment, turning the book around in search of some explanation.

"Can we see her, please." Stephan was now growing impatient.

The WPC handed the open page to the liaison officer

whose eyes stare in bewilderment. The WPC led them into the back of the ambulance where a green-faced Sam was grinning at them.

"Where's Charles?" she harped.

Simon looked around and then sat on the end of the trolley. "Sorry, he isn't here. He is still there looking for you."

Sam looked into his eyes and then into Stephan's. "No," she wails. "We were that far apart," she sobs, gesturing her hands to measure the distance of half a meter. "He was sitting next to me... how?" She started coughing again.

"Excuse me," the medic pushed around Stephan to check the lines.

Simon chipped in, "The lines are fine. It's probably the mixture of opiates and amphetamines," he announced. "Oh, you bad girl." He waved his finger at her. "All that moonshine too. Your head a bit spinny?"

"Sorry, but can I do my job, sir?"

"Amphetamines and opiates?" the WPC enquired.

"Yeah, it's in that leather diary. I got the recipe for the mixture in there too. Dirty rats, aye." Simon giggled, leaning forward and pinching Stephan's bum.

Sam narrowed her eyes at Simon.

"You didn't?" she asked.

Simon grinned. Stephan shuffled about nervously, like a naughty school boy.

"As for you," Simon flapped, "you, up on the common!"

"*What?*" yelled Sam. Simon nodded. Stephan nodded. "That's personal!"

"He wrote it all down, this way and that, and you, you randy bugger!" Stephan laughed.

# THE MIRROR

Pulling the mask off, Sam put her hands over her mouth in astonishment and went bright red. Then she grinned. "He had the biggest cock ever," she slurred. "Fucked my brains out. Nearly split me in half. His cock was sooo big." She giggled again, her head swaying. "Never had a fuck like that! I can barely walk!" She continued yelling, giggling giddily.

The medic paused a moment before reprimanding her language and then commented, "You could have suffered internal injuries, miss, whatever you were up to. Let alone the lasting effects of the illicit drugs." The medic was shaking her head.

The WPC took back the diary from the officer and handed it back to Simon, rather sheepishly unable to make eye contact with Sam.

"You all read them?" Sam boomed.

The WPC chipped up, "You can all go when you're ready with the paperwork on this. It will be too difficult to explain the charges. But miss, please let the medic attend to you to make sure you are in fit health. And please come later to the station, as we may still need a statement for the zoo. How did you get in?"

Sam shrugged.

"It's the mirror," Simon rambled.

"*The Mirror* paper?"

"No, the mirror in her flat," Simon explained. "Time. Well, time; how do we explain time. What if we could go backwards as well as forwards and not in straight lines as we try to comprehend it. Why do old people and the very young ramble on about things that never really happened in their life? Are they remembering something from a past life? What if a past life could be folded into our so-called present life. And time – where does it start and end? Regressive hypnotherapy has tried to prove this, but what if it could be done in reverse. Would it change history? And where and who does that make us? Have we a choice in our decisions? Or are they already done?"

He pats the leather book and smiles softly at everyone's open mouths

The WPC shook her head, "whatever you guys are up to at the hospital its sure screwing with your brians!"

# CHURCHILL

Charles sat shivering in the police cell, awaiting his impending doom. His heart was stifled and heavy. He knew all too well where she was and was desperate to see her through the mirror, to find her again. Why had it taken her back?

The walls and floor were grimy grey tiles; he was cold, and his head spun with the onslaught of future events. He coughed a little and spat the bile on the floor to clear his throat. He was hunched over on the thin mattress. He twiddled his thumbs in anticipation. It was his second arrest since she had disappeared. The first was for her missing person, but he convinced the police in Hampstead that they had been out on the common foolishly frolicking in the hedge growth during a raid, and she had been wrapped in his coat for warmth when she disappeared. They put out a search for the girl and found empty shell holes in which they found some unfortunate remains and were unable to identify the body. They assumed his truth and sadness of the loss of his sweetheart.

Things soon turned grim when the cleanup crew went

into help restore his flat had found an unusual device in his room. It was a form of communications device, and now the picture was set that perhaps the girl was a spy and had disappeared with vital information. She had a strange accent and had been at the wharfs three days before the brewery was hit. Was he a spy passing on information? He worked closely within the government. He also had links to France and regularly sent parcels, money, and telegrams there.

Who was the girl? There was no record in the parishes of her, and her strange attire and attitude led to suspicion. He clutched his diary, the only thing he was allowed, apart from the Bible. He had scribbled many thoughts of her: their night of mad, lustful pleasure; how his heart missed her companionship; their conversations; them together. How was she somewhere in the future, so far away for him to reach her. But she had his diary, a comfort for him to know. That gave him hope to reach out to her.

This is what he wrote, and this is what the police officers were reading at the zoo:

> My dearest, sweet, golden-haired angel; I pray that you are well. I hope your hand has fully healed, and I beg of you to forgive me for any hurt when we were out on the common. I know that it was both foolish and selfish of me to entice you there and to fill you with a concoction of methyl amphetamines and opiates. And to have lustfully taken your body for my own pleasures. You are an amazing creature, sent from heaven itself to save my soul from impending misery. Now I have known true

# THE MIRROR

joy in the company of a true woman who has taken my heart and my soul with her. Oh, how I miss you, Samantha, Samantha from the twenty-first century. I found your time chaotic; I wandered streets, lost and not known where I was, who I was, and who the people around me were. I have leave of my senses, my heart and my soul aches, they yearn so much for you. I saw you briefly the day we went to the coliseum. You were home, surrounded by many people at King George House. You were giddy in want of me. I feel in my heart and I yearn in my heart that you feel a joined soul with me.

I fear that the police have found your so-called cell phone. It was in my flat by the balcony window. Now suspicion is rising; I am arrested for espionage. It pains so to sit here accused of such atrocities. My mind ponders why such an ill fate is to fall upon us. Only time can tell. In knowing this, I have done as you requested and appealed to speak with my good cigar ('chugging,' as you would say) friend. I am held in Charing Cross station, awaiting my meeting. I may not be able to write much more because they will read all that I have. I assume the worst penalty I can face. Who will believe my story of the magical mirror and its angel that came and saved a lost soul.

I loved you with all of my body that night. I wanted us to merge and be one soul in the stars forever. Forgive me and my foolish heart; I cannot bear to be without you, but when I die, I will know that I have held truth and happiness in my arms.

Samantha Tomlinson of 4 King George House. I am bewitched.

I ordered the flowers to be sent to your home some far time in the future as you requested. The shopkeeper seems to believe I am mad, but she agreed to keep her promise.

I miss you so much. I can almost feel you. I will always remember you and your mind so clipped, precise and full of hope despite your own tragic times. You have given me hope in knowing of our success against the Nazi regime. I hold that tight and secure in my very soul. Also, you spoke of Fleming and his amazing new drug, I will endeavour to encourage the man.

I can hear them approach. My heart will always be yours.

Charles xxxxx

Charles closes his diary for the last time. He kisses the cover and presses it to his chest, knowing she will one day be sitting reading it, a long time after he will be gone. The door clangs and the keys scuffle in the lock.

A foreboding, top-hat-wearing man steps through

the doorway, chugging heavily on an enormous cigar. He scans the room and then booms at the officer who has just unlocked the cell. He tips his hat to a full arm stretch to Charles. He then turns and booms at the police officer, "Get me a chair, damn it." The officer calls to his fellow for a chair. "Christ's sake," he commands. "This the King's physician, not a bloody murderer. Get him a coat. A clean one!" He poises in the door and steps boldly forward. The officer with the chair nervously enters, placing it down, making it screech on the tiles. "Give it here, boy," he says, snatching it away from the young officer's grip. The boy's eyes are terrified. "Now beat it." He waves his hand to shoo him. Then he winks at Charles, offering a cigar. Charles accepts it willingly, and for a moment, the two men sit in silence, puffing.

Churchill addresses Charles in French. "So, you bloody fool, what have you been doing?" Charles twitched uneasily. "I heard you got yourself tangled up with a mysterious woman." He coughed. "I told you to stay away from those bewitching bodies." He laughs haughtily.

The policeman still has the door open, perplexed at the language used in exchange. Churchill turns around and booms, "Shut the bloody door." The officer does so.

Charles leans forward and hands Churchill his diary. "*Gardez cette sécuritaire.*"

Churchill scowls at the book, but takes it from Charles. "*Leur sont choses dont je besoin de vous dire.*"

Churchill nods and continues in French. "You okay, man? Bloody fools can't speak English let alone French, but keep your voice down." He nods, making his jowls wobble.

Charles speaks, trembling. "You may think I am mad, but you must know. I promised to tell you, and then you will have to decide what to make of me. I am sorry, my friend." Charles clears his throat. "When you go to Carthage in Tunisia, you mast take Lord Mansion with you. You will become ill. It won't be Fleming's new drug that will heal you, it will be sulphates." Churchill smokes. He leans back on his chair, pulling something form his pocket – a small hip flask. He offers it to Charles.

"You bloody fortune telling now?" He chuckles.

"Like I say, you will think I have lost leave of my senses." Charles continued, coughing slightly with the rich, warm, burning liquid going down his throat. Charles notices his diary has been placed where the flask was.

"Stalin will try and force you to push the front back onto France in a D-day launch. But do it four days later than you originally plan; there will be a sudden weather change, and the radar systems won't be able to detect it."

"You know about the radar?"

"I don't know much, but I was told about Bletchley Park."

"You were told what? By whom?" he ordered belligerently.

"The girl, the girl." He points at his diary.

"You are being held on espionage charges, so why should I believe what you say?"

"You paint. Yes, no one knows about your secret passion of painting. You take them everywhere."

Churchill leans forward, making his tone softer. "Go on."

"Why would I betray someone I have stood next to in desperate times." Charles flicks his eyes back up into Churchill's. "I promised I would tell you what she said. She

# THE MIRROR

is from..." He paused. "The future. The great British future. She didn't tell me everything but just things for you to know, that you must know to beat the Nazi bastards."

"How did she get here?"

"She couldn't tell me."

"Mmm..." Churchill sat back, pondering the advancement in technologies and the truth. "Carry on, man. I don't have all day."

Charles was aghast at the very thought that Churchill was believing him.

"December of this year, the Japanese will attack Pearl Harbor and the Americans will have no choice but to join the Allies. It will almost wipe out their entire fleet that's based there. They will decode the Japanese's code, and the American Navy will push them back from the island of Midway. But the Japanese will take over Thailand and Burma, mainly due to strong aerial forces.

"Stalin will join the cause but only to benefit himself. Also, you will find that Stalin was the mass murderer of the missing Polish officers., It isn't t the Nazis." He continues, "Poland, well, Warsaw will be levelled to the ground by both the Germans and the Russian advancing army. It was the Russian secret police that massacred the Polish officers and buried the bodies in the Katyn Forrest near Smolensk. It's a real mess on that front. The war in the Pacific, the Japanese will surrender after the detonation of a terrifying new energy bomb designed by Albert Einstein. There's the massacre of the Jews in the concentration camps and the treaty of Versailles. But don't trust Stalin; he will want to keep his half of Germany. Don't believe Rudolf Hess, either. He is here to fire up Mosely's black shirts."

He glugs at the hip flask. He raises his head to meet Churchill's eyes. Churchill speaks quietly, low, leaning forward. "Can I tell you something, friend, without you repeating it to anyone?"

Charles nods.

"I believe you," he announces. Charles is stunned, his hands back on the flask. "I have seen her. Been somewhere. Somewhere, your home, but not."

Charles squinted, concentrating. "We were playing cards at your place, a few weeks back." Churchill clears his throat, giving a slight raspy cough "I was pouring myself a glass of that French brandy your mother sends you. Well, a sneaky glass." He laughs. "I know where you hide it!" He points to his nose, knowingly, smiling. "I was fumbling about in your locked cupboard, glimpsing in the mirror to see if you had noticed what I was doing. I had pretended to drop my cigar and then a very odd thing that happened." He chugged and slurped from the flask. "I stood up with a full glass in one hand, sneaking the cupboard shut. I was bemused in what I saw. A slim, tall, golden-haired maiden. She was clad in what I can only call something tightly embracing her curves, showing all he athletic figure. Only saw her for a brief moment as she past through the room. She seemed to have been exercising of some sort. All sweaty " He chortled, raising his eyebrows.

"But it was something else that intrigued me: the newspaper on the table. *The Daily Mirror.* Its date and typeface. I thought I was going mad. However, it had an article about me. Me!" he snorted. "So, I took the paper, tucking it as much as I could into the inside of my jacket. That's why you thought I had a second deck and was

# THE MIRROR

cheating." Churchill now points his finger at Charles. "I am a bloody good card player and need not cheat. I was the one who taught you, remember?" He grins. "You see, the paper told me everything you have told me and more."

He slaps Charles's knee and hands back the flask. " I destroyed the paper by burning it as soon as I had read it. And now it all makes daft sense."

Churchill puffs hard. "But the authorities know nothing of this matter and now I have a dilemma with you, my friend."

Charles sat back and winced. He nodded in accord.

"You know," he spat.

Churchill nodded. "To begin with, I thought I was mad, but you have confirmed all truths." He smiled.

"However, your association with Alexis Carrel, the contraption found in your apartment, the missing girl, the bombing of the Lion Brewery where the girl had been three days before, it's all a terrible coincidence.

"But you believe me, you said," Charles stammered.

"Indeed I do." Churchill passed back the whisky. "Tell me, how do I convince the legal system without jeopardising myself?" He gestures, waving his hand around the cell.

"*Merde,*" Charles whimpered, putting his hands in face.

"There is very little I can do for you, my friend. The case is too complicated to unravel a time traveller or time travel. Hell, perhaps we are all mad!"

Charles took hold of his nerve. "Please, keep the diary safe. She will need it."

Churchill nodded, tapping the side pocket. "Anything you wish me to add in it?"

Charles leaned forward to the request. "Tell her what

happens to me, please. But make it as painless as possible." His mouth is now dry from fear. "You have been my friend, and I am sorry for what you have to do. I know you cannot help me any more than what you will try. But take heed of all that I have said and what you have read. Sir."

The police sergeant is knocking on the door and enters. The conversation falls quickly back into English.

"God speed with you, and you will succeed."

Churchill stands, retrieving back his flask and adorning his top hat. The officer hands over a clean, warm coat for Charles to wrap around himself.

His eyes sadden at the last few words the two will ever exchange. He says, "I will keep my promise." He tips his hat to Charles. "*Tarif bien mon bon ami et fidèle. dans mon cœur, vous serez.*"

Charles stands and puts his hand across his heart. "*Les mêmes. Que Dieu soit avec vous.*"

Charles slumps back down on the mouldy mattress as Churchill disappears through the clanging doorway. A tear of despair rolls down Charles's face.

# THE BAG

They spent some time in the ambulance, and Simon convinced the medics to let them take the giddy blonde home and clean her up. The medic agreed and released Sam into the custody of her good friend and cousin. Stephan drove carefully to avoid the bumps and to annoy the bridge traffic. They pulled up outside the flats. Simon pilled through the main doors and was met by a grim-faced Uncle, who was holding a wooden box. Sam swaggered about like a rag doll, forcing Uncle to grab her under a free flailing arm. They stumbled up the staircase and only one nosey neighbour came out to see what the commotion was about at such an early hour.

Simon flumped the giddy Samantha down on the sofa and shyly suggested that she needed a bath and would go and run one. Uncle halted his action just for a few moments to consider the bizarre events of the past few days. Then Stephan rapped on the front door, and his face fell on seeing his father standing forebodingly by the fireplace.

" The chief executive of the zoo telephoned me with a rather odd happening to a member of my staff and family."

He boomed, placing the wooden box down in front of the fireplace. He pulled her tattered bag out of it. Sam's head whirled at the startling voice.

"Shh," she hushed him. "*Redelik, ek het 'n slegte hoofpyn!*"

"That's not all, young lady." he rebuked. "Can someone explain what Samantha was doing in London Zoo and taking amphetamines." He scowled.

Sam just kept shaking her head, waving her hands around. "So much noise," she bleated. "Blasts and bombs and crap and shit and god then him," she grunted.

Uncle scowled at her drunken retorts. "Him?"

"Oh god. yes. Him... he..." Simon jabs her. She grins.

Uncle was loosing patience; his face was red and extremely tense. But as he was about to launch into a tirade of medical expertise, he was stunned into absolute silence. A young man was standing with his back to them in the mirror. He was smartly attired but with what seemed to be a traditional evening suit hanging over one arm. The young man turned to face the audience and was as startled as they. Samantha bobbed her head up over the sofa and squealed in delight. Leaping over the furniture, she called his name. The other men were stunned. Stephan called out, "Oh my god, oh my god."

"It's him, it's him," Simon flapped, squeezing Stephan's hand in excitement.

"Blimey, what a looker." Stephan squealed.

Sam had a hold of the young man and squeezed her body tight into his, forcing her mouth upon him.

"God," she breathed excitedly, allowing the stunned Charles to gasp for breath. "I didn't think I would ever see

# THE MIRROR

you again!" She forced her mouth back upon him, kissing him with lustful hunger.

She could feel his arousal as she pushed her body as close as possible into him. Her uncle called her name, to let the man breathe with dignity, and she released Charles. As she did so, he disappeared as quickly as he arrived.

Samantha yelled at her uncle, "You made him disappear! You frightened him away! You bastard!"

She stormed across the room towards the bathroom.

"Samantha!" he called back after her. "I'm sorry."

Simon and Stephan looked candidly at each other and let go of their hands. Stephan paced cautiously across the flat to attend to a wailing Sam.

Uncle rubbed the back of his neck and then gazed at Simon.

"I don't know where to begin," he stammered awkwardly. "At first I thought it was one of your many practical jokes." Simon shifted from on foot to the other in discomfort and twitched at the wails coming from the bathroom.

"I'll show you. Maybe that will be an easier explanation." He knelt down and opened the bag.

"That's old?" Simon asked. Uncle nodded.

"It was found three weeks ago in the restoration of the old south wing. It had a note attached inside, and it's all a bit bizarre. It's been there hidden since 1942." He scratched his head. "Have a look. You may not believe it, but with what I have heard and just seen..."

Simon peered over his shoulder and gasped at the contents of the bag. Putting his hand amongst the faded colours and dust, he knew what he was seeing. "No, you're kidding me," Simon retorted.

Uncle shook his head. "I couldn't believe it when the workmen bought it to me... but it's the note... hidden within..."

Uncles eyes welled up. "I know the handwriting, and I have asked him about it. Although he denied knowledge of it at first, I showed him the note. He explained to me about the night at the coliseum in 1941 when a young, handsome doctor, a pioneering surgeon, lost his new lady during a raid out on the common. He explained to me that the doctor was so distraught and heady with opiates and alcohol that they searched and believed that the girl had fallen victim to the raid. However, the surgeon was later arrested and shot for espionage, as a listening device was found in his flat. This flat." He continues waving his hand about. "The girl's bag was left at the home of his future wife and, terrified they would suffer the same fate, they hid the bag in a box under the floor in the south wing, where the surgeon often stayed during long surgical procedures. The note was only a prompt of innocence, signed anonymously." Uncle coughed. "It's a bit of a weird one."

Simon sifted about in Sam's dusty, heavy bag, reading the note. The note stated: "Open this bag with weary eye."

"I believe you. I believe all of you. Now we need to get the girl sober. And say nothing yet of the poor man's ill fate," he warned Simon.

# THE SNOW

It was some time in the following week when Sam fully detoxed, feeling very sore and sorry for herself. She was fed up with the ongoing blood tests and visits to the gynaecological department. She had been too intoxicated to have been given the morning after pill, and the results were pending on whether she needed a scrape.

She had suffered bruising from her illicit sexual activities and need antibiotics for a mild infection. She was not allowed back on duty until they could be certain she had no blood infections. They tested for syphilis, gonorrhoea, AIDS, dysentery, and other vast, immense tests. She was sick of being prodded and poked, being reprimanded for the risk she put herself at. Being part of the medical team, she could receive a disciplinary punishment or lose her job.

Stephan had gone away to Moscow for the weekend and Simon had been sulking, putting down the phone on her. Blubbering on about Stephan two-timing him and using his body.

She posed several times a day, gazing in to the mirror, pondering the plight of the surgeon. She would twirl her hair, rub her hands across her stomach, sigh, and question the mirror. She would talk to it, begging it to bring her Charles to her, or her to him. Her heart was breaking within, longing for the companionship of Charles. She knew all too well how the pipe smoke had affected both their heads and wondered why he had taken such a drug to extreme length with her. Questions arose, but answers never did. On the fourth day, when not so sore, she requested permission to visit the library to see the diary again. Alas, she was not allowed on the premises, and the diary was once again under lock and key.

The discovery of her bag in the south wing had caused more heartache for her. The remnants were ragged, but the iPod still worked with a good charge up. A few items were missing, but that was no surprise. Her cosmetics, perfume, a small compact mirror and her eyeglasses were all absent.

Then it occurred to her to visit her great-grandfather, but word was out that she was in isolation. She managed to telephone him for information about what had happened to the great Nazi spy.

George, whose voice wobbled and stuttered on the phone, took his time to explain the disappearance of the young girl and the execution of the great doctor. She sobbed at the plight of Charles and doubled in pain from great despair.

Simon called round that evening, bringing the smuggled-out diary. Stephan had phoned him from Moscow to say that Sam had phoned George, their great–grandfather, and had been inconsolable about the plight of the surgeon.

Simon thought it would be comforting for her to read

THE MIRROR

the last few entries of the diary. It was a cold, chilly night, freezing, with the breath cutting and stagnantly hanging in the air. He wrapped up in the army jacket Sam had bought him earlier that year and donned his head with Stephan's borrowed kosak hat.

He was unsure in the doorway, but Sam welcomed the company of her good friend.

"The police came today, " she began, "about the charges against Johnnie." She rolled her eyes.

"Oh? And what did they say?"

"Well, WPC Gillingham gave a good record of what happened. The CCTV caught the moment. Apparently they clocked me throwing coffee over Johnnie. It could be a provocation of attack. But the damage he did to my hand..." She began to sob. "If it had not been for..." She wailed. "For Charles..." Simon shifted.

"I heard you spoke to your great-grandfather." He twitched. "Stephan phoned me."

"What ? How is that going to help? With the whole bizarre episode. All those people lost and forgotten and some accused, were not needed. Plotted, scapegoats..." she wept. "Me still here in my head, like yesterday." She pointed to her head. "O'Hara says it's like post-traumatic psychosis. But after all the tests, there is more to be done. I have an infection too. It's quite painful at times, you know." She sobbed.

Simon shook his coat, hanging it up, and clumped across the living area.

"It's cold in here," he commented, stoking the fire and putting more wood on it. "You'd best warm up. You're looking a little pale." He tried to smile sweetly with doe eyes.

"Anyhow," she piped, "how the hell did you seduce my cousin?"

He grinned, plunking himself down on the sofa next to her. "It was one of those things." He shrugged. "It was Stephan, actually, who made the first pass," he chortled.

"What?" She chuckled for the first time in days. "Yeah, right... Mr Charisma, wandering eyes."

"He has done it before, you know. He was hot. And randy." Simon chuckled "Here, I thought you should read this. It might be of some comfort to you." He handed over the diary. "Shh, I snuck it out. The other old lady was on duty; she took pity on you."

Sam held the leather book with shaking hands, and her tears fell onto the leather. "I'll go make some tea," Simon informed her, leaving her to read the last few entries in private. He boiled the kettle several times to drown out her sobbing.

He returned to the room, clutching some heavily buttered toast and sweat tea. Her head was drooping; the book was clutched against her chest; her shoulders were shuddering from the deep sobs.

Little was said throughout the evening, and Simon puts her to bed after she had sobbed herself to sleep clutching the book. Simon slept on the sofa in front of the fire, keeping it stoked up. It was an unusually cold night.

In the morning, Simon woke to silence, a soft, muffled deafness. The world was still and bright. Blurry eyed, he paced, shivering to the balcony window, gasping at the thick coat of white snowfall. There were no buses trundling along the bridge. The pavements were indistinguishable from the road. The river was calm and still. Simon opened the doors and drew in the sharp shards of icy thick air. Ah, it felt exciting to see London at a stand still. He bounced back across the room, stoking the fireplace, jiggling the logs and paper. He put back on his jumper and socks and padded into the kitchen.

Sam woke to the aroma of wood burning and the fresh crackle of smoky bacon and brewing coffee. Her room was alight with an eerie soft-white glow. For a fleeting moment, she believed she had been deluded over the past few weeks, but as she moved, she knew the reality of her soreness. She wandered slowly into the living room to a very overexcited Simon laying the table for breakfast.

"Look out the window," he flapped. "Look, look." Sam rubbed her eyes behind her spare set of out-of-date spectacles. "Go look, it's like a fantasy world." He waved her to the balcony window.

She padded over, peering out onto the silent world of London. She gasped, and a small pang of excitement rose in her.

"Wow, so silent. So still. So bloody cold."

Simon was beaming. "I'm glad I got Stephan's hat." He beamed. "Here, get this down you. Then it's snow fun!"

Sam nodded in agreement, and for the first time in a good week, she didn't feel guilty in stuffing herself full of the English breakfast. She quaffed down the freshly brewed sweet coffee. They grinned at each other and rushed to get themselves wrapped up for the bitter cold outside.

Sam grabbed her double layered Russian coat that Stephan had given her from his last trip to Moscow. They gloved up and excitedly cheered as they left the warmth of the apartment and stepped out into the brisk chill. Simon was first to launch a snowball, smacking Sam full on the shoulder. She scooped up a handful from the wall, pressed it as hard as her hands could, and lobbed it back at Simon, missing his head by inches. She took a deep breath and supped in the shards of chilling air. Oh, how good it felt to be alive and to witness London so clean, white, and quiet. It was the quietness that was eerier in its own powerful moment. Her mind raced back to the sight of the bombers leaving from the same spot where she had stood with Charles. St Paul's was still and poignant, dusted like a fairy cake. A cold splodge against her cheek slapped her back to reality, and she heard Simon's war cry of snow fight. He was racing away from her, slipping and tripping clumsily in the piled snow. She pursued him up over the bridge, and they both paused, absorbing the fantastic London whiteout.

"It's a fairy tale," Simon panted, his breath steaming through the air. "Never seen snow like this in London. Ever." He gleamed. "I wonder what your friends, the giraffes, make of this?"

Sam laughed and then bowed her head. Before her mood fell, Simon gave her a shove and started racing over the bridge and towards the city.

"Hey," Sam called, "can we go up to St James park?" Simon froze in his tracks. "Please. I won't go on anymore. I need closure."

"Christ, Sam," he boomed.

"Please, Simon. There will be very few people about, and I just need to."

He agreed on the grounds that he could throw as

many snowballs at as many people, including her, without reprimand.

"Honestly, Simon, you're a big kid." He grinned and began his onslaught, pounding her, tossing snow off the bridge. A passer-by approached cautiously but in the good fun an exchange of friendly fire.

They marched along the North Bank, stopping for a hot chocolate from one stall holder who had managed to bear the elements and opened to warm those who were brave enough to stretch their legs, determined to get to the office.

Simon commented that there would be a huge increase of broken radii in orthopaedics, as well as dislocations. He was glad he was off duty, but no doubt he would get a phone call later saying that they were be short-staffed in the A&E departments. He kept his mobile switched off just in case. Sam hadn't got a new phone yet and wasn't sure if she wanted a new one. It was hard work stomping along, and Sam noted the change in the buildings history.

They sauntered up to horse guards and both froze. Sam had the diary tucked up in her coat and felt a strange coolness trickle down her spine.

They could hear the soldiers inside calling commands and stamping their feet. They approached the gates and were greeted by a burly faced guard. Sam cocked her head at him. He looked odd, somehow. The lieutenant saluted her and opened the gate. She paused quizzically, looking back at Simon, who followed her in. The man kept talking, but Sam didn't understand what he was saying. It was all odd. She spoke back to Simon, who shook his head that he didn't understand either. She tapped the lieutenant on the shoulder and spoke softly that she had wanted to see the tiltyard. It was about an espionage execution. The man looked bewildered at her and politely requested she stay were she was. Sam didn't understand his words but acknowledged his jesting.

"Cor, it's got really cold," Simon complained. "What's that all about?" Sam shrugged her shoulders.

"It is cold. I'm glad we got these coats." She smiled. "You could pass for a Ruski looking like that," she teased Simon. She blew hot breathe into her leather gloves and jammed her hands back into her pockets. She discovered a folded piece of paper in one pocket and began to retrieve it when a few more uniformed soldiers dashed towards them.

They came forward and saluted. One pulled the paper from her hand and spoke in broken English, "You come for prisoner?"

Sam cocked her head. Why would a regent battalion officer be speaking in broken English? "We did not know you were interested? Please." He spoke hastily, ushering them through to the courtyard. Suddenly, Sam's heart thudded intensely; she suddenly understood.

Churchill lifted the receiver of his phone, nodded, and scratched his head. While he listened, he thumbed the leather diary.

He placed the receiver down and looked skyward through his frosty window and whispered, "God speed, *mon ami fidèle et conforme*!"

A single shot was heard echoing over the tiltyard of Horse Guards Parade.